"Do you believe in the afterlife, Mr Hazard?"
asks Goliath.

Mr Hazard responds nervously. "Well, it's a bit
of fun, isn't it? A lot of nonsense, really. Quite
frankly, when I'm dead I hope that's the end of
it. I really don't want to be loitering about
haunting someone, banging on doors and
making daft noises in the night, playing silly
beggars!"

"Have you ever seen a ghost?" I ask him.

"No, little girl, I haven't." He peers down at
me. "But I've witnessed some horrible things in
my life. Musical Theatre! Frightened the
buggery out of me."

The twins stare at me with their inquisitive
eyes, a thin smirk spreading across b___ their
lips, like a line in the sand drawn ____ __ __k.

"Hello," I say.

"Hello," they reply tog___ ___

I stare at the ge_____ ___ ___ ___nt
yellow hair. He has

"My name is John ___ __e says. His
eyes suddenly fix upon ___ ___nd what sort of
creature are you, little lady?"

• ISHBELLE BEE •

THE SINGULAR & EXTRAORDINARY TALE OF MIRROR & GOLIATH

from
THE PECULIAR ADVENTURES
OF JOHN LOVEHEART, ESQ.
VOL. I

ANGRY
ROBOT

ANGRY ROBOT
An imprint of Watkins Media Ltd

Lace Market House,
54-56 High Pavement,
Nottingham,
NG1 1HW
UK

angryrobotbooks.com
twitter.com/angryrobotbooks.com
Lions and tigers and bears oh my

An Angry Robot paperback original 2015

Cover and illustrations by John Coulthart
Set in Meridien and more by Argh! Nottingham

Distributed in the United States by Random House, Inc., New York.

ISBN 978 0 85766 442 6
Ebook ISBN 978 0 85766 443 3

Printed in the United States of America

9 8 7 6 5 4 3 2 1

For Mum x

Prologue

In the summer of 1887, my grandfather stole a clock. He trundled it out in a wheelbarrow and loaded it into a pony and trap, and off he went with a click-ity clop. A big smile stretched across his face like a chalk line drawn by a child on a blackboard, wonky and unsure.

    Click-ity clop
  The clock was six feet high
    Click-ity clop
and the shape of a coffin.

Those wicked time machines. Pyramid, coffin, clock… *click-ity-clop*.

  Smash up the clocks. Tread them underfoot, throw them at the walls. Break their faces, pull off their arms.

Stop clocks.

Stop the clocks.

Stop the tickety-tocks.

PART ONE

My guardian, the enormous, exotic and bearded Goliath Honey-Flower arrives like a star falling and imprinting the surface of the Earth.

тнUD

he has landed.

A galactic footprint.

The moon a stage light for his materialization onto the Liverpool docks. The sky is the colour of porridge and the sea, a miserable treacle black. It makes everything sticky.

I am his ward and my name is Mirror. My name is a reflection. A piece of the moon.

My hair is as red as paprika and I am bundled up in black bear furs. Goliath grips my hand and guides me onto the slimy surface of the dockyard.

Our captain, Mr Mackerel, is a white-bearded weathered old gent, with eyes like sea jewels. He deposits us on the docks with a wink and a crooked smile; like a demented midwife, delivers us straight from the sea. His strange, ragged cat gazes the shoreline for fat rats. I cuddled that cat like a teddy bear on the journey, feeding it bits of ham and stroking its orange fur as though it were a great tiger. It had eyes like magic beans, dark and chocolatey that looked at you and said, "I have my own secrets, you know. I am no ordinary cat." Captain Mackerel calls him a little bugger and shakes his fists but, I am sure, loves him as deeply as he loves the sea.

I think that is all that matters in this world. It does not matter what you are as long as you love and are loved.

We have travelled from Egypt and it has taken us months to return to England. We had been staying in Cairo with Goliath's father who is an archaeologist. He has been excavating a tomb of one of the Egyptian princesses.

The skies are gold and pink in Egypt and there are many gods. The skies in England are grey and pale blue and I am told there is only one god here but there used to be more. They have disappeared; swallowed up in stories. Left only words behind.

We visited the tomb of the Egyptian princess which was covered in drawings of blue beetles with horns and green fish with stars above their heads. Red flowers were painted on her skin and bursting like fire out of her mouth. The god in England is made of wine and bread, and his churches have pictures of grumpy looking men praying and angels with swords. I ask Goliath what the old gods of England were like, the ones who disappeared, and he tells me there were gods and goddesses, some of the river, of the forests and of the animals, and they would speak to humans in dreams and in the patterns of the stars.

I miss the colours of Egypt. I think about all those fire flowers of the princess and the little pots she was buried with. I got to hold them in my hands. They had tiny drawings of frogs on them and strange eye symbols. I wonder if she was some sort of enchantress, if she was something not from this world.

Captain Mackerel's little ship is called the *Mermaid's Tail* and it is painted as green as limes. As we stand on the docks I stare down upon it and say goodbye.

It bobs up and down on the grimy waters, overshadowed by the other vast metal ships without names or colour. It is raining heavily and great splodges of water fall into my eyes and Goliath's beard, disappearing like pearls thrown into a wild forest. He gives me a huge grin, showing many white teeth, and puts me upon his great bear-like shoulders, carrying me like a ship's mate up the mast through the crowds of grey and shadow-heavy people lurking about the docks. Seagulls screech like witches and the moon above us is shaped like a sickle. The people here wander about like ghosts, grey upon grey. That is how Liverpool appears to me. Not like London, where I grew up, which pulses with blood and dark magic. There is no strange glitter here. Captain Mackerel waves goodbye, holding his soggy cat in his arms. I will miss them both and, I am sure, will never see them again.

We make lodgings at a tavern called the Drowned Sailor, deposit our bags and head off into the night to Quack Alley. Goliath has arranged a meeting with a gentleman known as Augustus Nightingale (whose real name is Timothy Scudfish – Goliath tells me he changed his name to sound mysterious). Mr Nightingale is a Psychic Medium, which means he can talk to the dead. People pay a lot of money to see him. Goliath tells me that he is well known throughout England for helping people who are possessed by demons and he is able to perform exorcisms. Goliath hopes he will be able to help me because something is inside of me, like the red flowers inside the princess. Something that is not human.

Goliath holds Mr Nightingale's book, *The Secret Knowledge of the Spirit World*, in his hands. He read parts to me on the boat. Mr Nightingale was born in Puddle Lane and his mother and father had owned a pie shop and he worked there for most of his life until one day, while serving pies, he said an angel came into the shop and told him to become a messenger of the spirit world. I remember that part because Captain Mackerel had been laughing so much he had nearly trod on the cat. Mr Nightingale, much to his parents' displeasure, had quit the pie industry and started to attend spiritual churches throughout Liverpool, passing on messages to the families of the dead, and had started acquiring a large following. Captain Mackerel said it sounded like nonsense and that Mr Nightingale was as psychic as a dead haddock. He said the only thing you can trust in life is the fish in the sea because they know all the secrets of the world and they keep quiet.

Quack Alley smells of something dead. The moon above us illuminates our footsteps. The street twists snakelike around a series of courtyards and behind a brick factory.

With some trouble we soon locate number 63 in a terraced row and Goliath knocks heavily on the front door. We hear the scamper of rat feet on a roof and the door creaks open, revealing a young boy.

"I am here to see Mr Nightingale," Goliath says, softly.

The boy replies, scratching his nose, "He's upstairs doing his magic tricks. He's a funny bugger."

The house is small and candlelit. A small framed photograph of a ghoulish-looking grandmother watches us from the landing. Skin stretched over a skull; pinpricks for eyes.

The stairs creak under the weight of Goliath; he can only just squeeze onto the landing. I follow behind and the little boy's eyes watch us all the way up the stairs. Mr Augustus Nightingale manifests onto the landing from the darkness like a pantomime magician.

"Welcome. Welcome. Come on in." His teeth are catlike: little and pointy. The only source of light is a solitary candle which flickers and jiggers, casting apparitions on the walls, which dance around us. In the middle of the room a woman sits on a chair. Her eyes are vacant and she gazes emptily at us. Goliath moves towards her and puts his hand on her cheek very softly. Mr Nightingale is grinning like a school boy. "It's a wonderful specimen."

"Specimen?" Goliath questions.

"Oh, yes. A quite powerful demon. I've never got so close to one before. Usually I deal with the low level ones. Minor tricksters, nuisances really. But this one, it's really something special."

Goliath stands next to Mr Nightingale. He is three times as wide and a foot taller. The floorboards ache under his movements.

Mr Nightingale points a shaky white finger towards me. "So this is your ward, eh?" He approaches me and examines me carefully. "Yes, I can see there is a problem with her. Something quite insignificant. I'm sure I can get it out of her. If you'd both like to stand over there you can observe while I deal with this higher level demon."

Goliath takes my hand and we step into the soft darkness and quietly watch. I could imagine Captain Mackerel throwing some fish at this man and swearing. Mr Augustus Nightingale is as thin as a broomstick, his long black cloak painted with elaborate golden thread symbols. His face is imp white with grey wisps of hair on his head and little shiny blue eyes that twinkle like oyster pearls underwater. He moves towards the chair and rests his hand on the woman's forehead.

"I command you evil spirit to leave this woman and return to the dark realm from whence you came. Go back, go back vile one." He mumbles some jumbled Latin and waves his free hand theatrically. Nothing happens. Mr Nightingale repeats his lines. I look at the woman, as though I am gazing through a peephole. I can see what is inside her. It is sadness. It is not a demon.

Mr Nightingale shrieks, "Begone! I command thee!"

I can feel that sadness, like a black ribbon; it is threaded throughout her. Goliath squeezes my hand softly, with love.

"I think Mr Nightingale is full of shit," I say to Goliath.

She is crying now. Crying over her life, her loneliness, in fear of the picture of the woman, whose eyes watch her day in day out. I think, take that picture off the wall and throw it away. Throw her away. She is with the dead, now.

Mr Nightingale, hysterically excited: "I command thee. I, Augustus Nightingale, Spirit Talker,

Command Thee. Return to thy wicked Master!"

I hear a smash from downstairs.

The woman has shut her eyes. Mr Nightingale laughs triumphantly. "I have saved her. The devil is gone," he cries and stands as though waiting for an applause.

Goliath moves to the woman's side and helps her up.

"Thank you," she says to him.

Mr Nightingale quietly says under his breath to us, "She was lucky. Sometimes the spirit is too strong for them to survive. Tonight has been a triumph." His eyes move to my guardian, nervously. The young boy creaks open the door, peering into the gloom.

"Mum, are you alright? Grandma's picture fell off the wall and smashed and I think the cat shat himself."

Mr Nightingale turns towards us. "I am performing at the spiritualist church on Duck Lane tomorrow night if you would care to attend. I could exorcise your ward on stage in front of an audience if you would like?"

Goliath shakes his head. "I do not think so Mr Nightingale."

Mr Nightingale looks down at me. "Maybe she

would like it. What is your name, little girl?"

"Mirror," I say.

"Would you like me to take the nasty demon out of you?"

"I would like to see you try," I reply.

And so it is decided.

We leave number 63 Quack Alley and return to our lodgings. The stars are now hidden under a blanket of smog and the air tainted with cat fuzz-stink. I wonder how much money slippery Mr Nightingale has asked for. I wonder, if he tripped on his cloak and fell into the harbor and drowned, would it be such a bad thing? Would the angels sitting on the rooftops intervene? Or would they shrug their winged shoulders and watch him sink underwater?

As soon as my head hits the pillow I am asleep. I dream that Goliath is an Egyptian prince and I am his magic crocodile with shiny, shiny teeth. I could eat anyone I wanted and he would let me do it.

The morning shines with an egg-yellow sun over Liverpool, the skies steel grey, with swirls of industrial cotton wool puffs. We eat bacon for breakfast with heaps of buttered toast. I lick the fat off my fingers and smile at the beautiful Goliath. His great dark beard has silver streaks like moonlight and his eyes are chocolate, deep and delicious. Today he wears a big fur hat and a great fur coat. He looks like a giant grizzly bear and I, his cub. By his side is a long silver cane with a frog engraved on the top. I asked him, once, why he had picked a frog and he said it was because frogs grant wishes if they are kissed. And so I kissed him on the cheek and made a wish that he would never leave me and would always, always love me.

Mr Nightingale is performing at the spiritualist church tonight and so Goliath has decided for us to visit a tarot reader during the day. She is called Nettie Stout, and she resides in a little shop on Goodhop Lane. She has been recommended by the wife of the tavern owner who had brought us up our breakfast.

We spend the morning feeding seagulls near the docks and we find a little bakery and buy meat pies for our lunch, followed by sticky buns. Goliath devours three and then announces he is going to buy me a book for our train journey the next day. We find a little secondhand bookshop, small and dark and stuffed with books. I like the sound the pages make when they are turned, the different colours and pictures. I like the smell of them, musky and covered in fingerprints.

The shopkeeper eyeballs us suspiciously, for we make a strange twosome. I choose a book of fairy stories with dark illustrations and a moral verse as a warning for children, which I think is funny. *Do not play with matches. Do not go for walks in the wood alone. Do not talk to strangers because they might be a wolf in disguise.* I hand it to Goliath, who flicks through it, pats my head and hands it to the shopkeeper.

"Red Riding Hood would like this book please."

I treasure that book because it is full of magic and wonder, like him.

Our appointment with Miss Nettie Stout has arrived. She is a pawnbroker but reads tarot in the backrooms, mostly for her neighbours and the odd visitor. She is a plump widow and her eyes are green as peas. We sit in the back of the shop, while Nettie shuffles her tarot. Goliath lays the money on the table for her. She quickly puts it away in a drawer, then continues shuffling those bright coloured cards.

"How long have you been reading tarot cards?" Goliath says.

"Since I was a child, sir. My mother and grandmother had the gift. My grandmother was a gypsy. Same colour hair as you, miss."

Nettie lays the cards out in a strange cross pattern

with a few random ones dotted about. They are well worn, tattered but bright like butterflies. Rich jewel colours. I want to touch them and reach my finger out but Goliath pats my hand away.

Nettie examines the cards carefully, raises an eyebrow and looks directly at Goliath. "You are a very wealthy gentleman. You are as rich as a prince, but you have never lived the life of a prince. You are trying to help her; you are trying to find someone who *can* help her. I am not able to. You must keep her away from clocks and mirrors. She has power over them. But I do not know why. I keep hearing insects ticking around her, like tiny clocks."

She stops. "I am sorry. I can't seem to get much for you both. It's the noise of the clocks. It's muddling my thoughts." She looks at the cards again. "You came over water on a little boat, a long journey from a beautiful place that you both miss. You will return there in the end. I can't get anything else."

"Thank you," Goliath says gently. Nettie's eyes glance at me.

"I can see the gift in others. Tea leaf readers, ghost talkers, dowsing with apple tree rods. I can see their light, it shines a little brighter than others. But I have no idea what you are little miss. You are something very different."

"Tell me," says Goliath, changing the subject. "Do you know of Mr Augustus Nightingale, the spiritualist?"

Nettie rolls her eyeballs and laughs, a deep warm chuckle. "I know cat turds with more psychic ability than that man. He's a ham bone, born for the pantomime."

"I am afraid we thought as much. We are seeing him tonight. Perhaps we shouldn't go."

Nettie smiled. "I used to know him when he worked in the pie shop. He was a creepy little fellow back then, but harmless enough."

We leave the little shop holding hands and go back to our lodgings, where Goliath reads me the fairy tales from beginning to end.

When we arrive at the little spiritualist church, people are stuffing themselves in like sardines in a fishing net. A great poster of Mr Nightingale hangs over the door, posing theatrically, holding a transfixed white owl that looks stuffed to me. The writing above:

The Gateway to the Spirit World can now be Open.
Augustus Nightingale,
Master Spiritualist

A small stage draped in black velvet, with a giant

eye painted in silk, adorns the centre of the room. There must be about fifty people here; all begin to seat themselves. Goliath and I select the back row to get a good overall view of the spectacle. Goliath has brought a bag of vanilla bonbons and some aniseed bullseyes to suck during the performance. My hand rustles in the bag and I drop a bonbon into my mouth. The lights dim and the audience stops nattering and adjusts themselves and all eyes gaze upon the stage. The giant gold silk eye shimmers and out he steps delicately, tiptoeing with fairy steps and bows, a low deep ascent, his cloak sweeping like black waters around him.

"Welcome, all. Tonight, I, Augustus Nightingale will invite the spirit world to communicate with me and depart messages to those amongst us. I would ask you all to be quiet, to help me concentrate, for I am the channel to their world, and it requires a great deal of my energy to maintain the link."

"And so we begin." He steps light footed around the stage, whipping up air under his cloak and with one hand rested on his brow and another pointing to the ceiling he cries, "Come forth spirits this night. Use me as your conduit. Give these poor people some advice. Aid them during this dark age. Enlighten us with your wisdom."

His eyeballs freeze into a trance-like state and he sighs a long, feminine sigh. He steps towards the front of the stage. "Ah yes, I can sense a man's name: John. There is a message for John." Three men stand up, presumably all named John. Nightingale points to the largest of the three. "You sir, within one full year you will be afflicted with the gout. Take measures to prevent this sir. No more puddings and pies. Listen to the spirit world. You may sit down." And so he does.

Nightingale gives a little whimper while Goliath hands me another bonbon. Nightingale points at a very elderly lady in the front row. She has some troubled standing up but holds herself steady with the back of her chair. She must be nearly a hundred years old.

"Madam. I sense your mother is in the spirit world." At this remark Goliath bursts into laughter and has to cover his mouth up with his hand. He swallows his bullseye in one mighty gulp. Nightingale thankfully ignores him and continues, "Madam, I have a message from your mother. She says get yourself a cat to keep yourself company. And she'll see you soon."

Poor Goliath's eyes are watering with laughter and I give him a cuddle. He is a big soft bear. He is *my* big soft bear.

Nightingale eyeballs a young boy near the edge of the stage. "You, young lad. Sometimes you hear bad noises at night. Say your prayers and be good. For you are hearing the ghosts of your grandparents wander about."

The young boy scratches his head. "Me granny is still alive sir."

"Yes, I'm still alive!" an elderly voice cries from the audience.

Nightingale moves backwards and moves a leaver attached to the side curtain, a puff of smoke and several black ravens fly out of the side. "They are the messengers of the other worlds." One flies onto the ceiling beam and craps into the audience. The audience claps.

Nightingale speaks, his voice excited. "Tonight there is a young lady in the audience who needs my assistance. She has a demon within her and I am going to exorcise it from her."

The audience looks curiously about the room. Mr Nightingale points in my direction. "Young lady, please come onto the stage."

I stand up and walk through the audience onto the stage, looking back and catching a glimpse of Goliath. He is anxious. Mr Nightingale stands next to me and I examine his sequinned silver moon cloak. A thousand tiny fingers have embroidered that cloak. The fingers of a fairy seamstress, such minute needlework. It is quite magnificent close up, and shifts like black liquid, dribbling elegantly like ink over the stage.

"This young girl," Mr Nightingale continues, "came to me for help. A dark spirit resides inside her. It speaks to her. Tonight on this very stage with the assistance of the spirit world I will draw that demon out and free her."

The audience claps, transfixed by the charlatan.

"Right, little miss." He waggles a bony white finger under my nose. "Stand very still." He positions me in the centre of the stage like a statue, whilst the wooden floorboards creak theatrically under his footsteps. He waggles his finger again, this time somewhat violently.

"I command you, spirit of the underworld, leave this girl's body."

The audience mutter and shift in their seats. I gaze out at them. A sea wave of faces mesmerized with Mr Nightingale, eyeballs popping like boiled eggs. Goliath, huge, standing at the back and watching me, rather concerned. I can see Mr Nightingale fumbling pathetically with his cloak, whilst mumbling some nonsense incantation. My eyes drift lazily to the side of the stage where the dead wait, quiet as church mice. They all start to smile at me. It is the wrong sort of smile. The dead are like photographs hanging on the wall. I wonder why they are here. What do they want? I want to send them back to the land of the dead. I think about fire, flames as red as dragon scales to make them disappear. I imagine the audience turned to charcoal matchstick men.

Mr Nightingale continues. "Hear me, foul spirit," and at this he rests his hand on my head. "Leave her and return to the foul pit from whence thy came."

The floorboards squeak under his feet. The dead are chuckling to themselves, whispering. One of those ghosts says, "I'm embarrassed for him. Some sort of brain damage," and he taps the side of his head.

I think about the Egyptian princess and her flowers of flames. I imagine her lying in her tomb, love charms placed at her feet, the hearts of birds put in little pots for her. All those hearts for her. And then I hear the screaming.

The curtain behind us is on fire, flames dancing up the walls. Mr Nightingale shrieks like a child. "How? How has this happened?"

I have no answer for him.

Goliath thunders down the aisle, throwing spectators aside. His great paws lift me up and carry me through the audience to safety outside. I see the ravens fly out of the church doors, followed by great lumps of people panicking and screaming onto the street. I can see Mr Nightingale putting out his beautiful cloak, which is flickering with flames, with a dirty puddle. A raven cackling at him, amused, from a nearby rooftop.

As Goliath carries me through the streets I keep thinking about Egypt and the orange moon at nights. I can hear Goliath's heart beating like a great clock. His father had a voice as rich as butter and was as big and dark-skinned as Goliath. I remember his hands, which were covered in ink stains from his writings on the tomb of the princess, his obsession. I remember the long conversations they had together, while drinking black coffee that smelt of syrup and the honey cakes we all ate, sweet and delicious. They would talk about the symbols painted on her tomb – the dung beetles, the magic eye for protection, the birds with rainbow wings – while the lemony sunlight drizzled over them. Those colours of Egypt were so deep and startling it was as if they had painted over me like oil on a canvas. Smeared into my veins.

Tonight, Goliath brings up mugs of hot chocolate and sits in a great armchair, cuddling me.

"Become a bear," I say.

And so he does. Around me are huge furry arms with claws, which squeeze. His snout is wet and his mouth displays many pointed teeth. Softly he growls and I fall asleep on my great bear. The smell of hot water bottle fur and his great heart beating lull me asleep.

I dream that Mr Nightingale is stewed in a pot and served up to the seamstress who embroidered his cloak.

II

Whitby
THE SÉANCE WITH MRS PIGWITTLE

The train heaves and splutters to Whitby like a great beast through the moorlands, juddering and shaking. The morning air is crisp and bright and the moorland wild, ghost-haunted and dotted with electric blue wildflowers, like the eyes of imps. The sky is lapis lazuli blue, the colour of Goliath's waistcoat, which is embroidered with forget-me-nots. His great hands grip a copy of *The Times*, the front page in bold lettering reads:

JACK THE RIPPER SENDS LETTER FROM HELL TO BAFFLED SCOTLAND YARD.

"Who is Jack the Ripper?" I ask.

Goliath looks at me carefully, peering over the newspaper. "He's a very bad man."

I stare out onto the moorlands. I can see a fox, the same colour as my hair, running through the grasslands chasing a rabbit. I put my finger to the window as though I am touching it.

"What does he do that is so bad?" I say, still staring at the fox, whose teeth now sink into the rabbit.

"He kills women," Goliath says quietly.

The train chugs past the fox. He becomes an orange speck on the horizon.

"Why?"

"Because he enjoys it," Goliath says sadly.

I jump on his knee and cuddle him, squashing Jack the Ripper in the process. "I love you. I love you, I love you," I say, snuggling into his beard. The train pants and shunts along, shaking us like eggs in a basket.

It is then I think of the word love and remember my sisters are both dead. I think about my grandfather, the one who went mad, the one Goliath rescued me from. It seems like another world and yet it has only been a year, so Goliath tells me. When I think of my past I feel I have been awoken from deep sleep,

a

magic

little

coma.

I remember only pieces of my former life, like a half-done jigsaw puzzle. My name was Myrtle and I had two older sisters, Rose and Violet. We lived with our grandfather in a small terraced house in south London.

My grandfather worked as a butler in a great house for a Lord. While grandfather was at work, we were looked after by our neighbour Mrs Bumble, who had nine children and was pregnant with her tenth. We called her Bumblebee, because she wore a great yellow dress with black stripes and was as round as a ball. She had a sad and dreamy voice and was the kindest woman I have ever met. She would hold us in her arms and tell us the secret ingredients to her cakes and spin us round and round until we were dizzy. Her children were plump and pink and buzzed around her as though she was their queen, and all of them were boys.

I remember she would rescue worms and spiders, cupping them in her hands and putting them somewhere safe. Sometimes she would sing to us, her voice sad and fluttery like wings, or make us cakes with cream and jam in the middle and then wipe all our mouths with a damp cloth before grandfather came home. She liked us because we were girls. Her hair was the colour of honey and her eyes dark and sharp like burnt sugar. Full of sweetness.

One evening grandfather brought home a huge clock. He said it was a grandfather clock, so it was made for him. It was taller than grandfather and had a great face painted on it with impish-black eyes that moved from side to side, watching, smiling and chiming every quarter of an hour. Painted and coiling all around the clock were ladybirds: black and red and shaped like tiny hearts. I tried to touch them with my finger, but grandfather slapped my hand away.

"Do not touch! It is a very special clock."

My grandfather loved that clock. He loved it more than anything. It sat in our front room next to his chair where he smoked his pipe. And he would sit for hours on end and listen to it ticking. Listen to its soft heartbeat. Rest his head against its wooden body, press his ear next to where its heart would have been. I wondered if it was stuffed full of angels beating their wings, trying to get out. There was something inside, something waiting.

A few days after he brought the clock home he

told us he had been dismissed from his employment. He said that the Lord who he had worked for had disappeared and a new gentleman had taken over the house and no longer needed servants. He said we shouldn't be worried about money because he had some savings and the clock would save us all. We didn't understand what he meant.

I asked him, "How will the clock save us, Grandfather?"

And he answered, "I have told you it is a very special clock. Never question me again."

And so now we spent every day with Grandfather and no longer saw Mrs Bumble. Everything changed. We used to go to church on Sundays with Mrs Bumble and her family. Grandfather would march us out in little white dresses with our shoes all scuffed, wonky bows in our hair. We would sings the hymns and listen to the vicar give long and fumbling sermons about forgiveness and wickedness, his long finger tapping on the pulpit, his great tongue lapping in and out. He had a weedy smell, as if you lifted up a rock by a pool and put your nose close to it. The church was made of cold grey stone with an enormous painting of Christ crucified, a weeping woman at his feet. Around him were a group of men who looked too puzzled or stupefied to move: they just gazed at him dying.

"He died so we might live," the vicar would say.

I wondered if Christ preferred the company of the dead.

Grandfather didn't want us to attend church anymore. We were no longer allowed to leave the house. All day and night he would sit in his chair by the clock and listen. Listen for what, we wondered? The eyeballs of the clock moving back and forth, back and forth, ever watching and smiling.

I remember Mrs Bumble knocking at our door and speaking to Grandfather, and he told her to go away. He told her to mind her own business.

The night before I died, I dreamt I had turned into a ladybird.

When I woke up, I knew this was that last time I would see my sisters. I ran to the door to get Mrs Bumble to help, but the door was locked and the windows bolted. I screamed and Grandfather put his hands round my mouth.

He sat on his chair in front of the clock. He said that he had something very important to tell us. He said the grandfather clock was a god and had spoken to him during the night. He said that the clock wanted to turn us into ladybirds. He said he had built a wooden box under the bed.

He has gone mad, I thought.

He told my sisters to get into the wooden box. They were so frightened they did what he said, and then he nailed it shut.

He opened the clock and told me to get inside.

"No," I said. My sisters were screaming. The clock started to chime.

He picked me up and stuffed me inside the grandfather clock and locked me in.

I can't tell you how long I was in there. I remember thinking I was inside a stomach. I heard the beating of ladybird wings. I think I was being eaten.

After the darkness, time unravelled, deep, soft and black as ink. I became full of emptiness. It coiled into me like liquid, oozing through me, replacing me. Something was eating my eyes.

I remember hearing voices of men shouting and banging. I remember trying to cry out but my voice was gone. I remember the door of the grandfather clock opening and sunlight as bright as fire burning my face as I was lifted gently out by a policeman, whose name was Goliath. I was five years old and all my sisters were dead.

My grandfather was arrested and committed to an asylum. It was Mrs Bumble who had gone to the police and demanded they do something. If only you had gone sooner, Mrs Bumble. My grandfather claimed at his trial that the clock whispered in his ear. Said terrible, dreadful, wonderful things to him. He said he had no choice.

Goliath was a detective with Scotland Yard, then. When he carried me out of the grandfather clock, I begged him never to leave me. I screamed when he left my side, even for a moment. And so he stayed and vowed to protect me from that day forth. And he has kept his promise.

We arrive at Whitby station. Orange and brown butterfly wings dance over the hedges at the platform. We grab our bags and shuffle outside where great puffs of steam billow out of the train.

"I'm hungry," I say, and Goliath grins and produces sausage butties from his bag and hands me one. I sink my teeth into it as a vampire into a human neck; delicious!

We sit on a bench and I can hear the seagulls crying, and smell salt and smoked kippers. My nostrils suck it all in. I love the smells here. Goliath tells me that we are going to be visiting a lady called Mrs Florence Pigwittle. He says that Mrs Pigwittle is a medium and she performs séances. He hopes she may be able to help me. He says that she is a celebrity of sorts and apparently has made contact with Lord Byron and Napoleon, and one of her guests last year was Arthur Conan Doyle, who praised her spiritual gifts. He seems sad when he tells me this; he doesn't want to let me down.

I give him a big cuddle. "You are the bravest man in the world, Mr Goliath Honey-Flower and I love you." And his smile is enormous.

We head through the streets of Whitby, passing the smoked kipper shop whose occupants hang upside down, dead eyes following us. The fish remind me of Captain Mackerel and his cat and I imagine them in their little boat exploring the oceans of the world, searching for mermaids. We wander past a cake shop with gypsy tarts and sticky buns. Goliath's dark skin and huge size attracts some attention from the locals, and an old woman mistakes Goliath's silver cane for a trident and declares him the God Neptune come from the sea. When we get to the beach, we sit on a large rock and feed the seagulls with pieces of cake from Goliath's pockets.

The sun lowers itself, and we sink into starlight on the mile walk to the Pigwittle Estate. I hold

Goliath's big hand. When he was in Scotland Yard he won many medals for bravery. He saved a little boy from a fire and tore down a door and part of a wall to reach him. When he carried him out his beard was singed black and his hands burnt. His hands still have those marks from the fire lines etched into him like an artist's drawing, and I love those lines.

It was he who found my sisters dead under the bed and he said it had broken his heart. I imagine him carrying them in his arms, like Egyptian princesses, and covering them in moon flowers and daisies. Safe in his arms. When he arrested my grandfather he told me that he had nearly broken his neck with his giant hands he was so full of rage and sorrow; other police officers had to pull him off.

I wish he had done it. I wish he had done it.

The path to the Pigwittle estate is lined with small yellow flowers and strange weed grasses that shift in the wind like strands of hair. We see two carriages move past us through the gates, carrying guests for the dinner and séance. The first carriage is pulled by two great big brown horses and carries a handful of guests, laughing and chatting colourfully. The second carriage that follows is smaller, pulled by two beautiful black horses whose manes and tails are decorated with purple feathers. Goliath watches carefully as it passes. We both sense something strange about the occupant of that carriage. A white-gloved hand rests on the window ledge.

We wander down the path. The house is impressive, with many red lanterns hanging outside, containing little flames dancing like tiny devils. Goliath knocks on the front door, and an elderly butler opens it and examines us with interest.

"Goliath Honey-Flower and Miss Mirror."

The house is full of the exotic and strange: Persian carpets, dark eerie paintings of weird and wonderful ancestors, a great stone Indian elephant, a hand of Fatima encrusted in gold and hanging on the wall, a wooden shaman mask with white painted teeth and red lips and black snake hair. Wonderful, curious things.

We follow the butler into the dining room, where a fireplace roars and the guests are already seated, engaged in conversation. At the head of the table sits Mrs Pigwittle, the famous Spiritualist Medium. She reminds me of the tubby children in fairy tales who get fed sweets by the witch and then put in the oven. Rising from her chair, she approaches us; I notice her feet are slippered, with a pearl dangling off each silk-shod toe.

"Welcome Mr Honey-Flower and Miss Mirror."
Her eyes ghost blue, her little plump hands shake
mine. "Lovely to meet you. Do make yourselves
acquainted with the other guests. The séance will
begin after dinner."

There are two empty seats. We sit down to
complete the party. Four other guests are seated
round the dining room table, whom we are
introduced to. First, a bushy red haired gentleman
and explorer who has recently returned from South
America is seated next to Mrs Pigwittle. His name is
Rufus Hazard. He has a medical background and a
fascination for unusual botanical specimens and
their uses in poisons and remedies. He reveals his
yellowish teeth through a fuzz of red moustache.

"Same colour hair as me," he says to me. "In
Peru they kept touching my hair. Thought I was a
devil, I'm sure they would have kept you as some
sort of pet."

Sat alongside Mr Hazard are Sophia and Clarissa,
who are identical twins. Bird-like faces with pale
coloured hair. Mrs Pigwittle explains that they are
able to read each other's minds and read the
thoughts of others.

And finally, a curious looking gentleman with
bright lemon coloured hair, which is sticking up on

end as though as he has been electrocuted. And he's wearing a white waistcoat embroidered in red hearts.

"Do you believe in the afterlife, Mr Hazard?" asks Goliath.

Mr Hazard responds nervously. "Well, it's a bit of fun, isn't it? A lot of nonsense, really. Quite frankly when I'm dead I hope that's the end of it. I really don't want to be loitering about haunting someone, banging on doors and making daft noises in the night, playing silly beggars!"

"Have you ever seen a ghost?" I ask him.

"No, little girl, I haven't." He peers down at me. "But I've witnessed some horrible things in my life. Musical Theatre! Frightened the buggery out of me."

The twins stare at me with their inquisitive eyes, a thin smirk spreading across their lips, like a line in the sand drawn with a stick.

"Hello," I say.

"Hello," they reply together.

Mr Hazard waggles a finger at Goliath, "I tell you, anyone breaking into song for no god damn good reason should be shot!"

"That's a little harsh, Rufus," Mrs Pigwittle chirps.

"It's not harsh enough, I tell you. I'd flog them

before I shot them!"

I stare at the gentleman with the bright yellow hair. He has ink-black eyes.

"My name is John Loveheart," he says.

"Nice to meet you, Mr Loveheart. My name is Mirror and this is Goliath, my guardian."

"Indeed," he replies.

Mr Hazard interjects. "Loveheart. What's your opinion on Musical Theatre?"

"I believe your idea about flogging is an excellent one."

"Good man. Glad to see there is someone of a sound mind in the room."

"Are you a spiritualist?" Goliath asks.

Mr Loveheart replies, "No, not at all, but my employer is interested in such matters. Or should I say, he is interested in people with peculiar talents."

"And who is your employer, if I may ask?"

"A man I'm sure you'll meet very soon."

The twins say in unison, "He's a very bad man, a very bad man."

Mr Loveheart's eyes suddenly fix upon me. "And what sort of creature are you, little lady?"

The twins reply, "He thinks you are very interesting."

"I don't know what you mean," I say. He looks

like something from a fairy tale. A prince of some sort. But something has happened to him, something wrong.

A spicy tomato soup is served with bread and butter. I sit opposite the stony faced twins, who slurp their soup in delicate, cat-like licks. Mr Hazard points out a shamanic cloak hanging from the wall, with feathers and bells, which is next to a skin drum painted with a red snake upon it. They are beautiful things. I think it is sad that they are hanging on a wall. Mr Hazard, who is keen to impress the young ladies, blathers on at some length about his recent tour of the Americas, and the variety of poisons used on arrow tips to paralyze enemies.

Mr Hazard's eyes are clearly wandering towards the two young ladies, who are both barely of marriage age.

"Fine pair those two," he mutters under his breath. Florence Pigwittle turns her attention towards Goliath. "I read your letter, Mr Honey-Flower, with great interest. And I will endeavour to see if I can help your ward in any way that I can. The spirit world may have a message for her."

Goliath nods with appreciation.

The twins chirp together, "Oh, Mr Hazard, you can't make up your mind which one of us you prefer."

Mr Hazard smiles, a little embarrassed, and goes on to explain about his meeting with a medicine woman who regularly drank blood and who had tried to eat him.

"Rufus, I beg you, you are putting me right off the tomato soup!" Mrs Pigwittle tuts.

"My apologies, but I feel I must finish this story. I escaped from that woman's clutches by wielding the stuffed human foot she kept as a weapon."

"Oh, for goodness' sake, Rufus!" the hostess gasps.

Dinner is roasted duck, potatoes, cabbage and beetroots. I lick my fingers of delicious duck fat. Our host tells us ghost stories during the main course while we gobble down the duck. There have been sightings of no less than three ghosts in the house. Mrs Pigwittle's dear mother, Prunella Pigwittle, her cat, Mr Fudge, and a disgruntled servant who had accidentally fallen off the roof.

Mr Loveheart's eyes wander while the stories are told, over the shamanic cloak and then onto me. Eyes like black holes. Eyes of a blackbird. On the other side of the table Mr Hazard is still trying his best to impress the young mind-reading twins with a tale of how he narrowly escaped an enormous crocodile by hiding in a swamp for two days.

Mr Loveheart suddenly speaks. "Let's play a little game." His voice is like tiny bells. A delicate warning.

Florence twitters, "Oh, I love games."

"Let's test the twins," Mr Loveheart continues, "let them tell us all our favourite food."

Heads nod and Mrs Pigwittle claps her hands excitedly. "Come on girls, we will all think of our favourite foods and see if you can guess."

Clarissa and Sophia stare at the hostess. "Marzipan squares."

"Yes, yes," she cries.

Their eyes dance to Mr Hazard. "Roast beef, bloody."

Mr Hazard bows his head in appreciation. They look upon Goliath. "Apple pie and custard."

Goliath looks nervous. They turn towards me, faces like a pair of birds, eyes small and sharp. "Chocolate bonbons." I clap my hands. And then they turn all the way round to look at Mr Loveheart. "Jam tarts."

Mr Loveheart grins. "Excellent, girls. Really well done."

The pudding is brought in: a huge steaming treacle tart with cream. Goliath has three helpings and I wipe my sticky lips on my napkin.

Mr Hazard wipes cream from his lips. "I think we should play the game again. This time let the girls guess our worst fear."

The girls gaze simultaneously at Mrs Pigwittle. "Being denounced a fraud."

They examine Rufus. "Crocodiles."

They look at Goliath, who is peering fruitlessly at his plate for the last morsels of treacle tart. "Not being able to protect her."

They look at me. "The grandfather clock, *tick tock tick tock*," they mimic.

They turn finally to Mr Loveheart, who looks directly at me. "It's her you fear the most."

We all remain silent for some time, until Mr Hazard slaps his hand down on the table. "Well that was delicious. When does the séance begin, Mrs Pigwittle?"

Mrs Pigwittle stands, "Of course, follow me into the library. We've got it all set up. I've a rare brandy, gentlemen, if you fancy a glass."

We are directed into an impressive room where a skull sits as an ornament on a circular table. The expression on its face is one of amusement. Candles flicker softly, shadows creeping up the walls.

"Ooooh, spooky," the twins sigh, excitedly.

We are seated around the table, Florence Pigwittle

placed gently next to Mr Loveheart. The skull's eye sockets flicker gold. Goliath is sat on the opposite side of the table from me, next to the twins. He winks at me.

The lights are dimmed, our shadows stretching like witches' fingers over the walls. We are told to hold hands, to be quiet and let Florence concentrate. I grip Mr Rufus's big fuzzy hand, and he whispers "Time for the ghouls to come out and play, little one."

Mrs Pigwittle sighs deep uncomfortable breaths and then slumps back into her chair. She opens her eyes, which are white orbs of the blind; her voice not her own, but something distant: *"There's somebody dangerous in the room."*

Mr Loveheart removes a pair of scissors from his waistcoat pocket and stabs them into her neck. Blood sprays across the wall and the faces of the twins. Goliath stands up, pulling the table over, trying to grab him, but Mr Loveheart is too fast and leaps over the table and grabs me by my hair and and drags me to the door.

The table is thrown across the room. There is screaming and chairs are being knocked over. I cry out for Goliath.

I bite Mr Loveheart Sink my teeth deep.

A terrible roar sounds; Goliath has turned into an enormous tiger, his tail a flickering whip, his teeth massive. He lunges at Mr Loveheart, who releases my hair and I am flung to the floor while the pair of them crash through the window and out into the garden.

"Good god!" I hear Mr Hazard shout as he lunges for the fireside poker to defend himself, while blood drips from the walls. I run to the shattered window and peer into the darkness. I can see nothing.

III

The Dream
THE TWELVE DANCING PRINCESSES

Once upon a time there were twelve princesses and they were locked in a tower. None of them were beautiful and all of them would befall terrible fates. Their names were:

Myrtle who was small and scared of clocks

Rose who kept falling asleep

Violet who dreamed she'd never wake up

Nettie who was overweight

Clarissa who was only a reflection of her sister Sophia

Sophia who was only a reflection of her sister Clarissa

Florence who was agoraphobic

Maggie who was really a cat

Foxglove who wore a mask, for she had no face

Lily who was scared of food

Belle who was invisible

Rosebud who poisoned people

Mirror who ate demons.

One beautiful autumn evening when all the stars were in the heavens winking like pearls, a crow with a little tinkling bell around his neck arrived with an invitation for them all to attend a magnificent ball.

All twelve princesses were released from the enchanted tower and transported to the ball in black carriages with enormous horses that carried them all into the Underworld, where the King of the Dead was waiting.

The King's name was Mr Fingers and he sat on a throne made of antique clocks, which chimed every quarter of an hour. His palace was decorated with the wallpaper of moth wings and firefly lanterns. When the princesses arrived they were greeted by many princes of the Underworld, who took them by the hand and led them away. The King of the Underworld chose Princess Myrtle to be his wife and he placed her on his knee on his throne of clocks. She was so frightened she lost her voice and when she opened her mouth only moths flew out.

Of all the princes, the most beautiful of all was Prince Loveheart. He chose Princess Mirror for his own.

My name is Mirror and I am dancing with Mr Loveheart in the Underworld. I don't know what has happened to the other princesses. I can see Myrtle sitting on the knee of the King of the Dead. But where are the others? Mr Loveheart is spinning me around the floor. I ask him, "Where are the other princesses?"

He replies, "My brothers have taken them away, deep into the Underworld."

"What will happen to them?" I ask.

"I am afraid they will be all gobbled up. For there's nothing much else we can do with them but eat them."

"What about Myrtle?" I look over to her; she is frozen like a doll.

"The King of the Dead will turn her into a clock. She will become lost in his time."

"What about me?"

"I haven't made my mind up yet"

We dance around the great hall; we dance in spirals while the moths beat their wings around our faces. A soft furry kiss of wings. Mr Loveheart is dressed in red with hearts embroidered on his waistcoat. His hair is the colour of lemons. So bright. His eyes black as octopus ink. I think to myself, he's a wicked prince and I am not going to get out of here.

We dance and dance. My feet are starting to hurt.

There's a beating at the great door of the hall. And in arrives another king. Goliath Honey-Flower. "I am the King of the Stars and I have come for Myrtle and Mirror." He opens his great hands out to us both.

The King of the Dead will not let Myrtle go. My wicked prince holds me tight and laughs.

The King of the Stars says, "Let them go or I will tear down your kingdom with my bare hands."

"No," says the King of the Dead, and the clocks chime a quarter past, politely. I don't think any of us are getting out of this.

IV

August 1887
MR LOVEHEART & MR FINGERS

My name is John Loveheart and I was not born wicked.

When I was a child, I was taken away from my home by a demon. I was taken away to the kingdom of the dead. When I came back to Earth I could not look into mirrors, for my eyes were black. The colour of dead things.

I remember our house. It was like something from a fairy tale. A magical kingdom of a king and queen, and I was the little prince. I remember in winter the snow would cover the house like diamonds: glistening, supernatural light. I remember thinking how lucky I was.

On my seventh birthday my father returned from Paris with a telescope and a map pinpointing the stars in the galaxy. I remember that time so clearly, as he was hardly ever home. He stood with me on the balcony, his finger an arrow aimed at the heavens, naming every star.

"John, remember the stars. They are constant when all else falls apart. They contain the souls of man. When I die, I will be up there forever watching you, forever with you."

My father had an enormous collection of machines and contraptions, which he had acquired over the years and throughout the world. Each machine was an invention. Each machine held the possibility of time travel.

I was under the strictest instruction never to play with these contraptions, as they were dangerous and also expensive. To me they looked like strange and beautiful sculptures throughout our house. A spiked wheel engraved in symbols in the hallway; a mirrored black coffin-shaped box in the dining room, an Egyptian throne of gold that used sunlight as a source of energy in the conservatory, even a set of shrunken Pygmy heads and a lightning conductor on the roof. In my father's study was a grandfather clock, his prize possession. He had acquired it from a clockmaker in London: a very unusual clockmaker.

"This clock," he said, "is very, very special. It has something inside it. Something trapped in time."

"What is inside it, Father? How does it work?" I asked.

"The clockmaker tells me it will start speaking to me. It will tell me how it works."

I gazed at that clock; it was a beautiful and frightening thing. It stood over six feet tall with a great painted face, its smile demented. Ladybird engravings crawled up the sides. What worried me was that it was shaped like a coffin.

When my father was out of his study, I secretly touched it with my hand. It was warm and I am sure I could feel it breathing.

It became my father's favourite thing in the world. He loved it more than anything.

My mother had become mysteriously ill over the last few months and was confined to her bedroom, as she was too weak to move about. The curtains were always drawn in her room as the sunlight was hurting her eyes and gave her headaches. Many doctors came to visit, each prescribing different potions and remedies, none of which ever made her any better. Eventually the doctors stopped coming. It was believed she simply had a weak heart and must rest and let nature take its course. As Father spent most of his time abroad with business or in his study worshipping his new clock, she was very lonely, and only had me and her sister for company.

Aunt Rosebud lived nearby. She was a widower; a tall, stern woman with amber, reptilian eyes and a bun of black hair coiled on the top of her head. Every morning she would visit my mother, sit by her bed. Every morning she would bring her needlework, for she enjoyed embroidering biblical phrases onto lace, and every morning she would bring with her a homemade cake to cheer my mother up. Little comfort gifts.

One morning, before Aunt Rosebud's visit, I took my mother some snow-bells, which I had picked from the garden. The flowers were so delicate, like fairy bells, as white as whirlpools.

"Good morning, Mamma," I said, The room smelt of lavender and something salty.

She smiled and I kissed her on the cheek and put the snowbells into the empty vase by her bed.

"How lovely they are John. Thank you."

Around the room, the embroidered biblical phrases hung mounted and framed on pieces of lace. They were surrounding her. They were closing in on her.

"How are you feeling?"

"The same," she said, sadly. "Tell me about your telescope. What did you see last night?"

"Orion's belt and the Great Bear. They were very clear, very bright. And I saw a shooting star, which is good luck."

"Do you think the angels are up there John? Do you ever see angels in the night sky?"

"Not yet. But I will keep looking. Maybe the shooting star was an angel and he's coming to get you well again."

There's a tap at the door and Aunt Rosebud enters, steely eyed, holding a ribboned box.

"Good morning Lily," (she ignores me) "I have brought a walnut cake."

"That's very kind of you, sister; but I haven't much of an appetite."

"Nonsense, you must eat." And she glared at me, my cue to leave.

This time, when I left the room, I sat by the keyhole and watched and listened. I had never done this before. But there were too many of those biblical lace gifts. There were too many of her cakes. My mother was drowning in them.

Aunt Rosebud perched by the bed, her voice low and hissing: "Lily, dear. Will you not try some of the walnut cake I have brought?"

"No. Perhaps later."

"Just a little, Lily, just a little. It will help you get better. Good girl."

"It tastes funny. It tastes strange."

"Just eat it my dear."

That was all I needed to hear.

pOiSoNeR

When my father returned from Paris that evening, I went up to his study and I told him what I heard.

"And what are you suggesting, John, exactly?" he said, sitting at his study desk, half glancing at the grandfather clock.

"Aunt Rosebud is poisoning Mamma."

He looked at me for quite some time. I think he knew. And then he looked at the grandfather clock, its eyes shifting towards him.

"Don't be silly, John, and never mention this again." His eyes fixed upon the clock. I stood in the way between the clock and him, blocking his vision of this weird idol.

"Father, look at me."

My father's connection with the clock was broken, and he stared at me sadly. "You will never mention your ridiculous theories to anyone. It would break your mother's heart. Now go to your room."

He knew. He knew. He knew.

That evening I crept into my father's study and looked at the clock. I had thoughts of burning it, pushing it out of the window. I kicked it. I kicked it again. I looked into its great moon face. I am sure it was smirking at me.

I looked through my father's desk and I found a locket. A curl of black hair; my mother's was sunflower yellow. And a picture of a woman with dazzling eyes, slanted like an Egyptian princess, and a smile that curved like a scimitar. A wondrous witch-woman for my father.

There was no one to protect my mother, but me.

The clock chimed midnight and I went softly into my mother's bedchamber.

She heard me step in. "John, is that you?" A heap of books rested on her night table. I glimpsed *The Mysteries of Udolpho* and *Jane Eyre*. I stepped close to my mother and sat down next to the bed. "Mother, I need you to listen to me."

She stroked my face with her hand gently. "What is it, darling?"

"You are being poisoned by Aunt Rosebud. I have told father and he will not listen."

She looked startled for a moment. "No one is trying to poison me, sweetheart. You are so imaginative." And she laughed.

"Mother, please. You must believe me."

"Go to bed, John," she said sadly, and turned away from me.

And so I went to bed and dreamt that night that the clock was watching me, ticking softly. And I heard the hum of insect wings. Dead angels fell from the roof of our house. I ran to the window and I could see my mother dead and floating down the river, tiny snow-bells in her hair, drifting on the water. My father was locked inside one of his time machines, frozen forever. I was alone with the clock. The wings of the ladybirds were fluttering inside my head.

In the morning, Aunt Rosebud arrived, a new poisonous cake in her hands. I gazed at her from the top of the stairs and slowly descended, our eyes fixed upon each other. "Aunt Rosebud," I said. "Good morning. Why don't we all have tea and cake together? I will fetch Father from his study. It looks delicious."

She examined me carefully, her lizard eyes

ancient and full of spirals. "I'm sorry John, but your mother likes our visits to be private. She needs the comfort of her sister. Why don't you run off and play?"

I had reached the bottom of the staircase. She was trying to read me, to guess what I knew or thought I knew. "What kind of cake is it today?"

She smiled, a smile like the clock. It frightened me. "Lemon drizzle."

I could hear those insect wings humming. The clock was trying to communicate with me. I stepped away from her. I am not a hero. I should kill this woman, destroy the clock and save my mother. I am a child. I speak, my lips moving, my voice from somewhere else. "What poison is in it?"

She didn't answer me. "I will speak to your father, John."

Everything changed after that. I was confined to my room for a month as punishment. Before that month ended I was informed by my father that my mother had died. It was deep in the month of August and on the day of her funeral it began snowing outside, our house a fairy tale palace of white. It was so beautiful that my heart turned into glass. Broke into pieces. Cut up my insides.

The servants gasped at the weather and shook

their heads.

"This is witchcraft," said the maid.

The funeral was small. A solitary raven watched over the service. Its eyes were devil yellow. Snow rested on the ground, delicate and untouchable as polar bear fur. After the service my father took me aside and said he had found a tutor for me called Mr Fingers, who came with superb references. He would be arriving in the morning.

That evening the grandfather clock was stolen.

It was still snowing the morning Mr Fingers arrived, the air dancing with snowflakes, cold little kisses, a thousand tiny bites. He was short, with a pointy black beard and half moon black spectacles and his coat and waistcoat were decorated with ladybirds.

He saw me staring at his waistcoat and grinned. "Ladybirds are little witches." His mouth stretched impossibly wide into a demon dazzle of teeth.

The demon had come for the grandfather clock. He questioned my father and then he tortured him. When he still had no answer as to its whereabouts he stuffed my father into his obsidian sarcophagus. Shut the lid on him.

When the lid was finally opened my father was gone.

Floating in space somewhere.

He let the servants go; took over the house and stole my father's money. Sent out advertisements with a reward promised for information on the missing clock.

And he waited.

"I am your father now," Mr Fingers said.

I wake up in a plump, pillowed bed to see Goliath sitting quietly by the window, reading *The Times*. His great bear bulk blocks the sunlight, blanketing me in shadow. The darkness spreads out before me like a roll of carpet to stuff Cleopatra in. Roll her up like a sausage and dump her in front of a Roman Emperor, who'll unravel her whilst licking his lips and plucking a grape from its skin.

Goliath smiles at me gently. "Good morning."

"Is Mr Loveheart dead?" I say.

"No. I chased him away. Have some breakfast, little one. There's toast and honey."

I stare out of the window at the sea. We are in a fisherman's cottage. We are still in Whitby. An envelope rests on the table by the honey jar.

"What is that?"

"Mr Loveheart has invited us for afternoon tea."

"Why? What does he want?"

"He wants to talk to us both. He wants to negotiate."

I spread my toast with a big dollop of butter and honey. "I want to hear what he has to say for himself."

"Very well, then."

"And if he tries to hurt me, I know you will turn into a lion and eat him," and I stuff a large piece of toast and honey into my mouth.

Late morning, Goliath carries me up the steps to the abbey and tells me stories of sea imps and underwater worlds.

The skies are full of soft cocoon-like clouds and the air smells of salt and seaweeds. I stare out at the sea on top of Goliath's shoulders and it is as blue and as deep nightmares. "Do you think Captain Mackerel has found a mermaid to marry?"

"I think he has found two. And they catch fish and pearls for him. And he is very happy, and the cat has a pearl necklace and is very happy."

We arrive punctually at our tea and cake destination. It is the home of Mrs Foxglove who, Goliath informs me, has a collection of death masks and an interest in tea-leaf reading. It is a large green cottage looking over the sea on the cliff, purple flowers and ferns overgrown in the garden and a bronze fox head as a doorknocker.

Goliath knocks three times and a tall lady with long white hair and delicate tortoiseshell spectacles opens the door, eyes like bright blue periwinkles, her voice impish and light. "Do come in. Mr Loveheart is already here. He does love my cakes."

The cottage has low ceilings, which make Goliath stoop, his great bulk negotiating the corners and doors. The air smells of sea-flowers and something else, something sinister. Goblin green walls are the backdrop for Mrs Foxglove's collection of plaster of Paris death masks; there must have been hundreds of them, each with a different grimace and look of horror eternally fixed upon their faces.

We enter the sitting room, where more masks line the walls and an elegant table is laid with numerous cakes and a large pot of steaming tea. And there sits Mr Loveheart, in green velvet with red hearts embroidered on his jacket; he has a mouthful of cake and a big grin upon his face. He remains seated as we enter, while Mrs Foxglove pours the tea.

"Now help yourselves to cake. I have six sorts: Victoria sponge, chocolate, vanilla cream, lavender, cherry and almond, and Mr Loveheart's favourite:

lemon drizzle."

Mr Loveheart continues to grin, while chewing his mouthful.

"May I ask how you two are acquainted?" asks Goliath, helping himself to the chocolate cake, an especially large slice, while I point to the vanilla cream.

"Mr Loveheart is a dear friend, as is his employer, Mr Fingers. They both help me acquire my beautiful death masks. So helpful. Clever boys, they are." And she ruffles Mr Loveheart's hair, playfully.

"Quite a collection you have," Goliath remarks.

"Oh yes, I have nearly five hundred. Hangings, decapitation, drownings – you name it, I will most likely have it. It's a fascination for me to see the human soul trapped in its final moments. The collection is very precious to me. They are my children."

"You really believe you have their souls?"

"Of course. They are trapped within the mask."

I look at the faces and lick my fingers of vanilla cream and think, she is wrong and she is quite mad. Mr Loveheart is staring at me, reading my thoughts and he too licks his fingers, gently mimicking me.

"Shall we get down to business?" he asks.

Goliath nods and Mr Loveheart, wiping the

remainder of lemon drizzle from his lips, continues.

"My employer, Mr Fingers, would very like much like to meet Miss Mirror, and suggested that the ideal location would be my ancestral home, this evening. A carriage will be collecting us after this delightful tea. My father, like Mrs Foxglove, was also a collector, although his obsession was time travel. I have invited many guests to view his machines this evening, with an interest to buy. They have been cluttering up the place for too long."

"And what exactly does he want with my ward?" grumbles Goliath.

"Well, she is of immense value to him due to a peculiar set of circumstances. You see, one of my father's prized time machines was a clock, which was stolen by your ward's grandfather, who I understand went quite mad and locked her inside it."

"And your point is?"

"Mr Fingers wanted the clock. Or, to be more exact, he wanted what was inside the clock. The man who made it was a most unusual fellow, and he had trapped a creature inside it. Some sort of deity (and he chuckled as if it were amusing to him). My employer finally acquired the clock through some inconvenience, but it is unfortunately now useless."

"Useless?"

"Yes, it seems that your ward has become the clock. The deity has been absorbed into her, become her. She was, I understand, essentially dead when she was taken out. The spirit of the clock has simply moved from one container to another – into her body."

"What does Mr Fingers intend to do with Mirror?"

Mr Loveheart rolls his eyes and drums his fingers rhythmically against the table, as though playing an invisible piano. "He would like to talk to her."

"And if we refuse?"

"You cannot keep running from us both. Surely you would like this situation resolved quietly. If you refuse, we will simply take her from you. You cannot protect her all the time. All he wants is a little chit chat."

Goliath stares deeply at Mr Loveheart and then rests his hand gently on my shoulder. "You and your employer are a pair of monsters. And I believe that you both intend to harm or kill my ward. It is true that this situation needs to resolved, so she can become free of the pair of you. I am her protector until the day I die."

"Understood."

Goliath turns towards me. "Little one, want do you want to do?"

"I want to meet Mr Fingers, and I want to see Mr Loveheart's collection of time machines, and I would like a piece of the chocolate cake."

"Are you sure?"

"Yes," and I don't know why I keep thinking, yes, yes, yes, yes. But it is the right answer to give.

"Then we agree to your employer's terms, Mr Loveheart," Goliath sighs.

"Super. We were going to drug the tea if you had refused, which would have been frankly impolite." Mr Loveheart pours himself some more. "I must say I was surprised and quite impressed with your little gift, Mr Honey-Flower. Your transformation into a tiger was quite unexpected. Satisfying, almost."

"Throwing you out of the window was very satisfying."

Mrs Foxglove, who had been dusting the death masks while we were talking, reseats herself. "Mr Honey-Flower, when you die, do you think your face will remain human or morph into an animal?"

"If you intend to have my face as part of your death mask collection then you are to be sadly disappointed."

She turns towards Mr Loveheart. "Perhaps, Mr

Loveheart, we could come to some arrangement? The usual fee, of course. I have a spot over the mantlepiece free." She looks towards Goliath, "It has a view of the garden."

"Madam, please. I intend to remain alive for quite some time," Goliath growls.

The small clock on the mantlepiece chimes, delicately. The death masks mutter amongst themselves. One of them speaks to me directly and I mouth the word "Aunt Rosebud."

Mr Loveheart looks startled. "What did you say?"

"Aunt Rosebud," I say again. The death mask smirks. "You should have killed her."

The death masks are laughing. Mr Loveheart grips the table; the teapot is shaking.

"Perhaps you will have a second chance."

Mr Loveheart composes himself. "Clever girl."

Mrs Foxglove gathers the empty teacups. "And now I shall read the tea-leaves – my other great passion. Drink up, Mr Loveheart."

Mr Loveheart drinks the remains of his tea and hands over his cup. She views her own first, turning the cup in her hand, examining the dregs. "Well, it seems a sudden and unexpected event is about to befall me."

Mr Loveheart takes out a silver pistol from his

waistcoat and shoots her in the head. She falls to the floor in a great heap, the lavender cake plopping off the table after her.

Goliath stands up, a protective wall in front of me.

"The lemon drizzle sponge was a little dry, don't you think?" Mr Loveheart remarks. "Time for us to depart."

Outside we can hear the arrival of a horse and carriage.

"You shot her because the sponge cake was unsatisfactory?" Goliath says, bewildered.

"Of course. I'm a connoisseur of homemade cakes, you know. Now come along," and he motions us to the door.

"You're insane," bellows Goliath.

"Of course."

The death masks watch us leave, happy as fat pumpkins in a field.

"I should warn you. My carriage doesn't understand the concept of time." Mr Loveheart adjusts his cuffs.

"And what do you mean by that, exactly?" asks Goliath.

"Step inside. Let's take a ride." He bows, playfully.

The carriage is lined with red silk, violent as a murder scene.

The horses scream, and we are moving – the carriage juddering, moving into darkness. The landscape morphs into a hell realm: the sea turns black with bloated corpses floating on its foaming lips. I see an angel fall out of the sky, black-winged and screaming. It lands in a heap by the road, bones shattering, giant wings a mass of blood and broken architecture.

"Whoops!" says Mr Loveheart, and shuts the carriage curtains, which are red silk.

Goliath holds me tight and glares at Mr Loveheart, waiting for an explanation.

"Short cut," Loveheart answers. "Spot of black magic."

Mr Fingers

I have no heart, so to speak. I am made up of dark matter and clock mechanisms. I tick, I tock. I have arrived from the underworld because I am looking for something. Tick tock. It is a very precious thing. It holds time, it holds something I want.

A god has become a clock. A clock has become a girl. A wicked little metamorphosis.

I am really quite hungry, now.

E
  a
    t

        E
         a
          t

E

    a

       t

Tick tock.

VI

Time Machines
AN EVENING AT THE HOUSE
OF LOVEHEART

We emerge from the darkness. Pink dazzles the
night sky as our carriage drives along the country
roads. It is the pink of Egypt; it sizzles. I think the
pyramids were giant time machines where the
King's body was transported to the Land of the Dead
and the black-ooze river of the underworld. I
remember seeing the burial chamber of a king and
his treasures found by Goliath's father – ostrich
feather fans, ebony statues, a solid gold sarcophagus.

Inside the tombs were magical maps to help the
King through the underworld, to help him pass the
demons who guarded the doorways. If you failed
the test your soul was eaten by a demon.

Why do those words make me think of Mr
Loveheart? Is he a king? Is he wandering in the
underworld on a quest to keep his soul? Wicked,

beautiful, mad Mr Loveheart. You are stuffed with hearts. They burst out of your eyes, fall to your feet like severed heads. Your guts are red ribbons. Your heart is a rose. I can see you, Mr Loveheart. I can see what he has done to you. He has murdered part of you. Buried you beneath deep earth, buried you alive.

You are a forest on fire.

Burn them, Mr Loveheart. Burn them all into nothing.

I remember the Sunday sermons I used to attend with my sisters. The vicar never mentioned magical maps or scarab beetles. He never mentioned the hippopotamus goddess or the crocodile god, the one who gobbled everything up. Instead, he would roll his eyes and point a long, pale finger at a statue of a man nailed to a cross. He talked about pain and hellfire. He talked about sacrifice a lot. I think that was his favourite word.

I bet the Egyptian priests would laugh themselves silly.

I remember the sermons on forgiveness. I remember the rain miserably pounding on the church windows. I remember the long sighs and much rolling of eyeballs of the vicar. I remember wishing he would drop down dead just so it would end, just so it would be over.

I think about those Egyptian priests, who have knives and mirrors in their hands, banquets and harvests, magic books of the dead, dragonflies in their ears and honey on their lips.

I look up at the sky; the pink is disappearing. Egypt is slipping away. I have been dazzled. I have been infected by it. When this is all over I want to go back there and lick the tombs of the pharaoh and dance with the priests.

Mr Loveheart leans over towards me. "Your name interests me very much. Mirrors are portals to other worlds."

"I would like to see other worlds," I say.

"Be careful what you wish for." He winks.

The carriage pulls up in front of the house of Mr Loveheart. It is a fairy tale palace. There are white turrets with secret, slitted windows, battlements for archers and banners, perhaps a princess locked in a tower waiting to be rescued. Other carriages are nearby: guests have arrived to view the machines of Mr Loveheart. I can hear music and laughter within, a rustle of skirts and the smell of cigar smoke. Goliath takes my hand as we enter the kingdom of the wicked prince.

An Egyptian mummy's sarcophagus perches in

the hallway, inspected by a monocle-eyed gentleman as round as an apple, a gentleman whom Mr Loveheart pats on the shoulder and greets enthusiastically. "Mr Orion, a pleasure. You like the Pharaoh?"

Mr Orion raises his bald head. "Really marvellous. What a treat. And you think this may transport me back through time to see Cleopatra?"

"My father believed in these objects and their power. I am simply grateful to be able to get rid of them."

Mr Orion says, "I am sure we can strike a deal." His monocle wobbles as he inspects the Pharaoh closely. "Perhaps I need to climb inside to be transported, so to speak?"

"As you wish, dear sir, as you wish," and Mr Loveheart manoeuvres us around Mr Orion into the sitting room, where a half dozen characters are viewing a great metal spiked wheel with a seat engineered in the middle, which rocks gently back and forth.

We are escorted towards a little room where the fireplace is roaring, and a small gentleman wearing little black glasses is watching the flames. Mr Loveheart leads me towards him. "There is Mr Fingers. Go and chit chat with him," and he gently shoves me in.

Goliath and Mr Loveheart stand by the door while I step closer towards him. Each footstep drawing me nearer to those flames, each footstep marked by the ticking of a clock. He raises his head slightly and looks at me, his voice rustling like leaves.

"It is a pleasure to finally meet you, Miss Mirror." He extends his hand towards me. I touch it and feel a thousand clocks tick tock, tick tock. Such immense pressure, my head hurts. I let go of his hand. The fire flickers like devil tongues.

"I went to visit your grandfather in the asylum."

I say nothing.

He continues, "We had a long conversation, mainly about the clock he stole. He knew what it was. He obeyed its instructions without question. Killed your sisters. How frail humans are, don't you think, Miss Mirror?"

"You are wrong. Goliath is strong."

Mr Fingers gazes at Goliath. "Your guardian. Mm hmm. He's not really human either, is he though, eh? He certainly gave Loveheart a surprise."

"And so here we are on this beautiful evening, the four of us in a house stuffed full of humans, curious about a collection of strange, useless artefacts that they believe can carry them across time. It's very funny watching them cooing over these metal contraptions as though they magical. They really are unbelievably stupid." He gazes at the crackling fire, "Do you want to know what your grandfather said about you, or should I say, your former self?"

"No, not really. I never liked him. I wish Goliath had killed him."

"Human relations. Another stupidity. Well, your grandfather told me you had turned into a ladybird. I happen to like ladybirds very much. He was of course completely insane."

I notice the ladybirds embroidered on his waistcoat, red and black and jewel-like.

"Do you like Mr Loveheart?"

"I think in some ways he is like me. Something very bad happened to him and has changed him."

"Ah," Mr Fingers sounds interested. "Do you think he is capable of redemption?"

"I think he has been poisoned. His heart has turned black. Maybe if he kills those responsible for hurting him, he can be free."

"A wicked prince in a fairy tale, under a curse. How romantic. Let me tell you a secret, Miss Mirror. He is both terrified of you and yet he loves you. And this is because you can see straight into what is left of his soul."

I don't know how to respond so I gaze at the floor, the sound of the fire crackling and bubbling.

Mr Fingers bends his head towards me. "You know this house is on the edge of London, the great capital of the world. The river Thames oozes past this great house, like a giant serpent. Do you like London?"

"It was my home. When I think of it, I think of my sisters. It makes me feel a great sadness. It is part of my past."

"It is my favourite place on the planet to visit. Full of magic, if you know where to look," he says curiously.

"I am tired of your questions. What do you want with me?"

"And now we come to that." He raises his hands to his chin, as though in prayer. "I want you to leave with me, tonight. Be a good girl and do as you are told and please me."

"You plan to kill me?"

Mr Fingers takes off his spectacles. His eyes are two black holes. It is like looking at a shark. "No. I plan to eat you."

Goliath has Mr Fingers by the throat, held up in

the air like a rag doll. He is choking and spluttering. I hear his neck break. Goliath throws him to the floor and picks me up in his arms and runs through the house. I look behind to see Mr Fingers rise up with the help of Mr Loveheart.

We cannot kill him. We cannot kill him.

We race past the huge metal wheel and then down a long corridor. Goliath kicks in a double door, which swings open to reveal a large chamber with a few guests, including Mr Orion, examining a series of contraptions: a mirrored coffin, an enormous metal chamber with cogwheels and a set of shrunken heads displayed in a cabinet. The room is a dead end.

We turn to see Mr Loveheart and Mr Fingers by the door. Mr Fingers speaks: "Miss Mirror, come to me."

Goliath looks around the room for an exit. He puts me on the floor and turns into an enormous wolf and leaps into the air. There's a tremendous shriek from the people in the room. The giant wolf sinks his teeth into Mr Fingers' neck, almost decapitating him. And then there is the sound of laughing and all is quiet and Goliath is no longer a wolf, but himself lying on the floor. Mr Fingers removes his hand from Goliath's chest, holding his heart.

Goliath is not moving. I run over and touch his face. "You cannot be dead," I cry. Something is breaking inside of me. Such rage. Mr Fingers towers over me. "Come with me, now. It is over."

I step back from him into the middle of the room. Mr Fingers raises his voice. "Do not be foolish. Come along, child."

I can feel those stupid metal contraptions around me, dead and unmoving. I can hear the shrunken heads, bickering, stuffed in the cabinet. I can feel the river Thames lapping around my feet. I can smell the blood on Mr Fingers' hands. I let the rage boil through me like electricity.

And the machines start to move. A clattering, a shifting of cogs and mechanisms, rusty and ancient. They are shifting and pulsing. The great wheel spins round and round. The glass coffin shatters into a thousand pieces. The cage is hit by a lightning bolt and judders into action. The shrunken heads are chanting. I feel the river Thames turn black and boil.

Mr Loveheart and Mr Fingers stand transfixed like statues, utterly speechless. The house is full of screams and people running. I look at Goliath's great body, lying on the floor and I say, "I am going to bring you back, whatever the consequences."

The time machines whir. Time shifts. Every window in that great house breaks. Energy moves through me. The house spins like a spinning top.

And then it is quiet. Goliath rises from the floor and carries me out of that house while rest of them are caged in time, porcelain statues, only able to watch us leave. I blow a kiss to Mr Loveheart as Goliath kicks open the front door to the house and we walk into the moonlight, the stars above us shimmering like diamonds. The house of Loveheart and its inhabitants frozen like mannequins on a stage.

VII *Whatever the Consequences*

In the deepest sleep I fall into the arms of Goliath.
Deep like the bottom of the sea. A magical coma. I
can't wake myself up.

*I am trapped in a dreamworld, locked up in the
grandfather clock.*

*I am lying on a bed in a forest. Beside me, the
grandfather clock ticks gently. His great eggy eyes roll from
side to side. The trees in the forest are deep and dark,
branches coiling, frogs croaking softly.*

*And I sleep and the clock ticks, singing to me its
mechanical lullaby.*

*After some time a little boy with hair the colour of
lemons approaches me. He is carrying some flowers.*

*"I picked these from the forest for you," he says. He is
small and shy. The flowers, tiny and blue and shaped like
stars.*

"Who are you?"

"My name is John Loveheart and I am lost in the forest with you."

And he sits on the bed with me while I hold the flowers.

"They are very pretty. Thank you."

Holding hands we walk into the trees, like Hansel and Gretel.

"Will you help me get out of here?" he says.

"Yes," I reply. The grandfather clock watches us leave.

We walk into a clearing where a little house made of sweets and chocolate stands. It looks delicious. Through the window I can see a lemon drizzle cake sitting like a golden treasure.

"Don't go in there," says Loveheart. "Do not eat any of it. A witch lives in there. It is all poisoned."

And so we continue, the smell of candyfloss under my nostrils, back into the darkness of the wood.

We come across Mr Rufus Hazard holding a rifle, pointing it into the trees. We approach him carefully, and when he sees us he smiles, big and beaming. "Well hello there." He has a big sack next to his feet.

"What are you doing?" says Loveheart.

"I am hunting," he grins. "Do you want to see what I have caught?"

We look into the bag. There is a dead girl in there.

"The other one has run away. But I shall find her."

"*Do you know how we can get out of the forest?*" *I ask him. Loveheart is frightened and stands behind me.*

"*Mmm, I can't remember,*" *he says, stroking his moustache,* "*but there is a lady sitting in a tree over there who may be able to help you.*" *He points in a rough direction and then lifts his rifle again, and so we leave him and walk over a carpet of lavender and moss and come across a huge gnarled tree with white death masks all over it. Mrs Foxglove, in a long, blue dress, is sitting on a branch, drinking a cup of tea. She stares down at us.*

"*Lovely morning, isn't it?*" *The death masks are chatting and she tuts at them,* "*Oh, do be quiet, children, we have visitors.*" *The death masks grumble.*

"*Would you like some tea?*"

"*No, thank you. Please can you tell us how to get out of this wood?*"

Mrs Foxglove looks puzzled. "*I don't understand the question, dear.*"

And so we leave her. And we walk for many hours, and eat berries and nuts, and drink from the stream. And we finally find a clearing where a traveling magician sits with a white rabbit in his top hat. It is Mr Fingers.

Loveheart says gently, "*That man is not my father.*"

Mr Fingers looks at me and says, "*Would you like to stroke the rabbit, little girl?*" *The rabbit, I notice, has black eyes.*

"No, I would not."

"Would you like to play a game?" He tilts his head slightly.

"No. How do we get out of this wood?" I demand.

"Little girl, there are consequences for what you have done. You have manipulated time. You have turned back the clocks. You have broken cosmic laws. Such action does not go unpunished."

"You are in no position to judge me, sir. You are a nasty little demon. And I have trapped you in time."

"Not for much longer," he sighs. "It is sad that we cannot be friends." And he pulls a bunch of fake flowers from his sleeve, hands them to me and laughs.

"What is going to happen to her?" Loveheart pleads.

"You will have to wait and see. It's a surprise."

VIII

Goliath & his Schoolfriend, Icabod Tiddle

I carry her as far away as I can. Miles across England, under a sack of space. Nowhere becomes, finally, somewhere – the home of my old school friend, Icabod Tiddle, the celebrated writer of children's fairy stories. I haven't seen him for nearly twenty years and Mirror is slumped in my arms when I knock on the door of his cottage in the Kentish village of Otford. It is raining heavily, the drops pounding the earth. And thankfully, after all these years, he recognises me and lets me in.

Mirror is taken to the spare bedroom, still in this strange coma, and I kiss her on the cheek and go to sit by the fire with Icabod.

His cottage is covered in scribblings and ideas for his stories. On the walls are dark ink illustrations of wicked witches and a prince trapped in a great forest. A selection of fairy postcards line the kitchen cupboards, each fairy performing a different task: singing, dancing, playing a pipe, kissing a frog. A great oak bookshelf displays his numerous published works, in both alphabetical and colour coded order. He is a stickler for fine details. He has the unusual quality of possessing skills of both imagination and order.

I had read some of his stories to Mirror over the last year. They were accomplished, perfectly crafted pieces with colour and wit. Little whimsical fairy tales for children. Pale moons hung over enchanted, fairy-kissed forests. Giants carried hedgehogs over magic bridges to safety. His landscapes were colourful, but more importantly, safe.

Icabod is a small boned, bird-like man with strawberry blonde hair and an impish little face, full of imagination and kindness. His eyes are small and green, the colour of frogs. He hands me a very large glass of brandy and pokes the fire nimbly. I am exhausted and slump myself in a great patchwork-quilted chair and feel the wonderful heat of the flames warm me, my beard still dripping with raindrops.

"Thank you, dear friend," I say, gulping down the brandy.

"You are more than welcome. It is lovely surprise too see you after so many years. I don't often get visitors, other than Mrs Spoons, who pops in for a bit of local gossip and brings me her homemade plum cake."

"I am sorry it has been so long. You are the bestselling author on fairy tales in England and, according to *The Times*, a national treasure."

Icabod looks kindly at me. "I have been extremely fortunate. I could have ended up a Vicar, as my father intended."

"You never married?"

"I was engaged briefly but she broke it off. She hated my stories. Said they were twaddle," and he laughs to himself, and then he looks at me, concerned. "Goliath, please tell me what has happened."

The fire spits and flickers. The fire poker, I notice, has a little bee on the handle. And the fireplace has engravings of imps dancing and butterflies. It is a lovely fairy tale world he lives in. There are no little girls locked up in clocks, starving to death. There are no demons. His world is safe and soft. If I could I would put Mirror into his world. But I fear it would not be able to hold her.

"Goliath?" Icabod leans forward. I had got lost watching the flames.

"I'm sorry. I am so very tired. I will tell you of what has happened, but first let me forget for a while. Tell me about your stories. Distract me."

"Of course. I am currently working on my ninth children's story. It is entitled *Horace and the Magic Foot*."

"The title is dreadful."

"Yes it is. But they will publish it, no doubt."

"Tell me the plot."

Icabod pours some more brandy. "Horace is an ordinary boy with a magical foot. His foot can grow extremely large, so he is able to kick in locked doors, stomp on wicked wizards and carry rescued maidens on it. One day, Horace grows tired of his magical foot because he simply can't fit in the world and feels odd and unconnected. Anyway, he comes across a wizard who offers him a deal: he will remove his magical foot and replace it with a human one if he will help him kidnap a princess. Now Horace agrees to this and kidnaps the princess for the wizard but falls in love with her and, well... that's really where I have got up to."

"Any ideas on an ending?"

"It has to be a happy one, of course. It's a fairy tale. What do you think?"

"I think I have missed you, Icabod. And the story is awful."

Icabod laughs out loud. "It is, isn't it? It's bloody awful – they all are really. I always wanted to write crime detectives stories, like Sherlock Holmes," and at this he lights his pipe. "Now are you ready to tell me your story, Goliath?"

"I fear my fairy story will not have a happy ending."

"How can I help you write a better ending?"

"You are already doing a great deal to assist me, and for that I am eternally grateful. I could think of no other place we could go, or anyone else I could trust."

And my eyes grow heavy and I feel myself drifting off into sleep.

I start to dream. I can see my father waving at me. In his hand is a little pot from the tomb of the princess. It has little green frogs painted on it. Inside the jar is a heart. He hands it to me.

"This belongs to you."

I wake in the armchair. Icabod has put a blanket over me.

"Good morning," he says sprightly. "She is still sleeping, but she seems fine." He hands me a cup of coffee and brings in a large plate of buttered crumpets. "Tuck in." And I do. I eat six and feel better. "Now," he says, "tell me your story from beginning to end."

And so I do, and for a long time Icabod says nothing, his eyes glazed over, deep in thought. The little clock chimes.

"What you tell me is extraordinary. You are not a man to make up such a story. I–" He pauses. "I believe you. But you must tell me, have you always been able to change into the form of animals?"

"No," I said.

"Then how?"

"It is Mirror who has changed me. The day I rescued her from the clock, she held onto me so tight, so tight. Squeezed me. And I felt it then, something passed between us. Some form of magic She gave me this power so I could protect her." And I took the last crumpet. Devoured it as though it were Mr Fingers' head.

IX

Death Pays Mirror a Little Visit

I wake up from my dream. Shout out for Goliath but no noise comes out. Only air.

Sitting on the end of my bed is a small boy with black hair with a silver pocket watch gently gripped between his fingers. He looks curiously at me. "You and I have a problem," he says. His voice is as soft as marshmallows.

"Who are you?" I sit upright, rubbing the sleep from my eyes.

"I am the last page in the book. I am all the endings. I am the collector of the dead. I am the father of time."

"What do you want with me?"

The boy spins the watch between his fingers. "You owe me."

He stuffs the watch into my mouth.

Time is fizzing, bubbles in water. I am melting.

When I wake up again, he's watching me carefully. His eyes are endless tunnels. "You have a great deal of power. I am not convinced you can use it wisely."

"I don't fully understand what I am."

"You can alter time, bend it to your will. You can open doorways to other universes. Do you realise how dangerous that makes you?"

I don't know what to say.

"Let me make something very clear to you. I can destroy you if I choose. You are not above the cosmic laws."

And we stare at one another. The pocket watch in my stomach ticks gently.

"I suppose I should say thank you for not killing me," I say.

"You're welcome, Mirror. It was most interesting to meet you."

I go downstairs, calling Goliath's name. The mirror in the hall shows my reflection. I have aged. Lost years.

I am no longer a girl. I have become a woman.

He just gazes at me, mouth open like a goldfish. And then he squeezes me so tightly, with so much love. The only noise is the clock in the hallway ticking softly, and I can't hear it.

In the house of Loveheart, the guests begin to wake. Mr Fingers adjusts his spectacles and walks out into garden, the rain pounding the earth. The gods watching him from above.

X   *Aunt Rosebud & Mr Loveheart*

I was not born wicked and yet I have become something wonderfully sinister.

I think I look rather fetching today: the mirror shows me a picture of a handsome man. But I don't really recognize him. Perhaps he is me. Perhaps he is something nasty. I do like my jacket, it is lilac velvet and very soft to touch. The devil is supposed to dress beautifully.

I am walking down the long path towards Aunt Rosebud's home. It is time I paid her a little visit. In my hands are an enormous bunch of flowers, violent purple and orange, a sign of my enduring love. She holds a special place in my heart. My heart, a cage hanging in an abyss. An iron birdcage. Maybe it's empty. Maybe I shouldn't think of such things.

I have passed the spiked gates of Crake Manor. No demon dog guards the entrance. No riddle to be answered. Should I be surprised? A great white house with a flowerless garden. Another emptiness.

I wonder about the conversation we shall have. No doubt she will remark upon my sanity, parentage and outfit. She doesn't like flowers, so the gift is inappropriate. Darling Auntie, are we the same kind of wrong, you and I?

Rat a tat tat!

A marvellously decrepit looking manservant opens the door.

"I have come to see my Aunt," I smile. Those magic words open the door, and I enter her domain with all my colour and my wicked flowers. Into a deep white space. I am walking on the moon.

I am escorted into the conservatory, leaving a trail of flower petals behind me. Visiting a minotaur in its labyrinth, I must of course find my way out again.

She stands erect and unmoving, a bible resting like a prop on the side table and a stuffed little dog in a glass case on the wall. Obviously her last pet. Maybe she has a glass case prepared for me? Stuffed and mounted on the wall. That would please her very much. Ha ha ha ha ha ha ha ha ha ha ha.

"Auntie," and I hold my hands out to the old dear.

She remains unmoved. "John, you look like a fool, some sort of clown."

"Oh Auntie, you old charmer," and I hand her the flowers, which she grasps rather wobbily and puts on her reading table.

"Frivolous."

"I knew you'd like them."

"You've grown up," and she paused, "You've been spending time in the company of devils. Why have you come here John?" She examines me coldly.

"I am your nephew and I haven't seen you in years. I've been thinking about you, Auntie. A lot," and I lower my eyes.

"You were always a ridiculous child. Spoilt by your philandering father. Ungrateful and ungodly. That stargazing contraption he gave you," (and she shook her head) "I told him it was a machine of the devil. Stargazing is ungodly. Unclean. Unnatural."

"Speaking of ungodly and unnatural, are you still baking, Auntie? Your walnut and coffee was a real heart stopper."

She says nothing for a while.

"You understand so little, John. I told your father you clearly had an underdeveloped brain, prone to excitement and imagination. You were always a little liar."

"Why did you do it, Auntie?"

"Do what, exactly, you little wretch?"

"Poison Mamma? I just want to know before I go as we may never see one another again."

"How dare you! I was the only one who stopped her suffering. She needed to be put to sleep into the arms of the Lord."

"And how many others have you put to sleep?"

"Dozens," she says softly. "Including my late husband, my children and my dog."

"I really have missed you, Auntie!" I cry happily and I pull out from my waistcoat a long silver curved sword. My voice lowered like a prayer, "We have so much to catch up on"

I chop her into pieces. A blood bath in the conservatory. And then I leave, whistling to myself.

The day shines a little brighter. The flowers bloom with a touch more colour.

Death & Mr Fingers Have Tea & Cake

If you look at me, you see a little boy. If you look closer you will see the universe floating in my eyes. Gaze of a surgeon, smile of a scissor shark. I am Death. I am the Great Collector. I am behind every closed door.

Today I am walking through the streets of London. The gentlemen in their top hats and elegant smiles stroll past me.

Black boils

Cancer

Muscle Spasm

Cholera

Syphilis

Heart Attack

Poison

Hangman's Noose

It is written on their faces. The letters thick and inky, imprinted on their skulls. Written in coils of time. Your fates are a teasing itch – you always want to know the outcome. Scratch it and see. London, city of poisoned water, sour milk, fish stink and shit. Blood bubbles and drips down the thighs of her. London: the bite of a mad dog, the kiss of a witch-woman. London: you eat raw flesh, dissect and arrange skulls. Mother: I know you from before. I have seen your face.

I have an appointment with the Lord of the Underworld. We are meeting in a tea shop down Dumpy Street. He's waiting for me, sits by the window of the winding, labyrinthine path. Smells of dead dog and boiled flesh down here. Mangled human beings, ragtag smiles and webbed feet, stare at me from the walls: huddled, hungry, sheep-yellow eyes.

Ladybird waistcoat, dark spectacles. Odd little man. I've never liked him. He reminds me of an autopsy: things have been removed, things are missing.

He nods as I sit down and pours the pot of steaming tea into little blue china teacups.

"So, why did you want to see me?" He peers over his spectacles and sips his tea. "I am rather busy at the moment."

"Did you order some cake?"

"No," he replies, rather annoyed.

I catch the eye of the young waitress, her hair the colour of roasting chestnuts, watery eyes, laudanum laced love-letters in her pocket.

𝔖𝔲𝔡𝔡𝔢𝔫 𝔥𝔢𝔞𝔯𝔱 𝔣𝔞𝔦𝔩𝔲𝔯𝔢

"Do you have any chocolate cake?"

"Yes, sir. Freshly made. Whipped cream in the middle."

"A very large slice, please."

Mr Fingers stares at me. "Well... I'm waiting for an answer."

"I am here to give you a little friendly advice."

"Oh really?" and he laughs out loud.

"Yes. You're playing with witches again."

"I don't know what you mean."

"The ladybird girl. You will leave her alone."

He looks surprised.

My cake arrives. "Thank you," I say, and bite into a large mouthful.

"Why do you care about this girl? What business is it of yours?"

"This cake is excellent, and chocolate makes me happy."

Mr Fingers pounds table with his fist. "Answer me!"

"You have always been prone to childish tantrums. It is one of your flaws."

"How dare you. I am the Lord of the Underworld!"

I rise from my seat. I lift a finger to the ceiling, as though pointing to heaven. Everyone in the tearoom drops dead. Falls like flies.

Thud

        thud

                thud.

He shuts up.

I sit back down and resume eating my cake.

"You're just showing off. Why can't I have her?" he says, annoyed.

"It will upset the natural balance of this world. You cannot be allowed to increase your powers. I will not allow such chaos."

"You're always spoiling my fun," he snarls.

"Why don't you have a piece of cake?"

"Fuck off!"

If you speak to me like that again **I WILL END YOU**

XI

September 1888
LITTLE WOMAN

I am a child woman. I look at my reflection in Icabod's hall mirror. I am tall. My face plain and pale. My hair bright and short like fire. Spiderweb lines on my face, delicate markers of my transition. And I look at Goliath, my protector. Things must change between us now. The love between us new and bright and frightening. I must protect him now. I touch his face with my hands. My pale hands against his dark skin and great beard. And we both know. We both know and we are afraid.

The three of us sit on the train to London. I am wearing a green dress and gloves which Goliath has bought me. It feels soft and alien against my body. It is the green of frogs and fairy tales. It is raining outside, the great black thickening rivers glittering like snake skin. Umbrellas open like black bird wings while the raindrops pound the earth. The world is becoming water.

Icabod reads *The Times,* gripping it like a holy parchment while Goliath holds my hand in his. The train chugs on like a tug boat, the Kentish countryside lush and rolling like waves. We are off to see an acquaintance of Icabod's: a hypnotist and psychoanalyst called Mr Edmund Cherrytree. He believes he can help me.

"How long have you known this man?" asks Goliath worriedly

"For about a year. We met at a book launch party. We share the same publisher. He's an odd sort of a man, but he has an interest in unusual patients and a gift to help them. He has an illustrious reputation and he seemed very interested in Mirror's situation and eager to see her." Icabod returns to *The Times,* eyes dancing over the headlines. "The Ripper still eludes Scotland Yard. It's a bloody disgrace. I fear it will end very badly."

"They believe he is a butcher or a surgeon," says Goliath.

"I don't think they know what he is," Icabod sighs.

Goliath says sadly. "He's clearly insane"

I think about the dead women of Jack the Ripper.

I imagine them lying on a table served up for dinner. I imagine Jack the Ripper with a knife and fork in his hands and a napkin resting delicately in his lap.

"What if he isn't mad?" I say.

"Then we are living in a kind of hell." And Icabod puts the paper down and stares out of the window, at a world sinking in water.

The train arrives at Victoria Station, the platform bustling with people, churning with soot and steam from the engines like a cooking pot. And we walk out into the great arms of London, into the capital of the world. The faces of the crowds are like a strange painting. An old woman is selling flowers on the street; she has no teeth and she stares at me. And I can feel the emptiness. A man is smacking a small child with the back of his hand and then spits, steam is rising from the streets, cracking open. Ready to burst. There is something red underneath London. It is the red of the flowers of the Egyptian princess, it is the red of Jack the Ripper, it is the red of a painter smearing oils on a canvas. It's on my hands too. I'm sure.

Mr Cherrytree's office is a short walk from the station. I can smell Mr Fingers, he's under the smog and the stench of horse manure, under the shadows and grime. In the dark corners, hiding and waiting.

He smells of something burning, like ribbons thrown on a fire. I think I can smell him on me. I'm not sure if I understand fear. I do not really know what it is anymore. And yet I know I should be afraid. I know what it smells like. It's the wolf in all those fairy stories Goliath read me. It's Jack the Ripper. It's the dark hole in that old woman's mouth. It's all around me. I am in the painting. I am in the red world.

We arrive at a very smart house on a bustling side street. The air smells smoky, hanging like a veil, concealing something, the sky as white as a shroud lying over the face of the sun.

As we enter the establishment we are greeted by Mr Cherrytree's assistant, a young, handsome gentleman who escorts us up to a waiting room. The walls of which are covered in framed spiritual photographs depicting the human soul leaving the body at the moment of death. Both eerie and fascinating, my eyes follow their trail around the room: an elderly woman lying face down in the snow, a wisp of ectoplasm rising like steam from her body; a soldier on a battlefield, eyes glazed, and again a wisp of soul emerging. Above Goliath's head, three sisters who have taken poison whilst taking tea lie slumped in their seats, an ooze of weird light seeping from them and floating to the ceiling. We are sitting in a tomb, on a dead white planet. The dead captured in photographs, like genies swirling in a bottle. And yet there is something wrong with the pictures, something off. Something empty.

Icabod looks a little nervous. "What ghoulish pictures. I do hope I haven't made a terrible mistake bringing you here."

We have no answer for him. Then in walks Mr Cherrytree, whose skin is as pale as my own. His beard as black as a fairy tale forest.

"Thank you for coming," he says, and looks at Icabod who rises and shakes his hand. His voice has a foreign accent, rich and deep with something playful underneath.

"Thank you for seeing us."

Mr Cherrytree approaches me, "Shall we get started?" and then looks to Icabod and Goliath, "If you could both wait here, we will be about an hour. My assistant will bring you up some refreshments." And Mr Cherrytree escorts me out of the room, as though leading me onto a dance floor.

Inside his office is a large brown sofa, which he tells me to sit upon. He perches himself opposite, like a great black bird. He is not at all handsome, his forehead egg-shaped and his teeth quite crooked: glinting, hidden within that black bearded mouth. I imagine he likes to look at himself in mirrors.

Stare into me. Ogle your reflection.

He likes what he sees. Mesmerizes himself in the glass. And today I am his mirror.

There are no pictures of the dead in here. Only an odd, beautiful clock on the wall, decorated with tiny snakes coiling like orange peel. There is something about this clock that is wrong, unnatural. It is an object of horror but I don't know why.

"Firstly, you have nothing to fear. I am experienced in dealing with, shall we say, peculiar cases," Mr Cherrytree says, revealing a glint of razor white teeth. "I need you to relax. Take deep, slow breaths." I do as he requests. He watches, perching on the edge of his seat like a crow.

"What if something goes wrong?"

He reaches across the table and picks up a little pink box, and, opening it, reveals chocolate truffles dusted with cocoa. "Take one and put it in your mouth."

I do. It melts on my tongue. He's a curious wizard, I think, luring little girls into his tower with sweets.

"Close your eyes, Miss Mirror," he says, and my eyelids shut like a book.

I can smell his breath: peppermints. "Imagine that you are walking down a long corridor and at the bottom of the corridor is a red door. You feel comfortable and safe as you walk towards this door."

I do not feel safe.

He continues, "You feel very light on your feet as though you are floating. You keep walking. The door is getting nearer and nearer until you are close enough to touch it."

I can hear the clock ticking.

"Open the door Miss Mirror."

I can see the red door. I can hear the clock ticking. I can smell the peppermint.

"Open the door and tell me what you see."

I turn the handle and I say, "I can see a big red butterfly. It is dancing in front of me. It is very beautiful."

"What is happening now?" His voice sounds far away, as though I am dreaming.

"The door has shut behind me. Someone has put the butterfly into a jar and it is dying."

I am sure he is stroking my hair. I can feel his fingers.

"What can you see now?"

"I can see you. You are taking a photograph of me

to add to your collection. You want me on your wall."

I am starting to feel unwell. I think I am going to be sick. I grip the side of the chair but I can't open my eyes.

"What are you?' he asks.

"I was trapped in a clock. I am inside a little girl."

I try to open the red door and get out. I try to open my eyes.

I can feel someone picking me up and carrying me. I try to shout out but my mouth opens and nothing comes out.

I am placed inside some sort of wooden box. I think I am inside a carriage. I feel the wheels move and the sound of horse hooves. I think he has put me in a coffin.

I scream the word *Goliath!* over and over and over. I can hear the windows smash. I can hear gunshots.

A bird is screeching in the air above us, following the carriage. It is Goliath. I know it is him.

My name is John Loveheart and I was not born wicked.

Tonight my ancestral home is full of demons. We are having a party. Isn't that wonderful! I have chosen to wear red velvet this evening, to match the decor. There are red banners hanging from the battlements, red candles and lush volcano red tapestries and carpets. My favourite colour.

The decor may be my choice but the guests are not. Mr Fingers has chosen them all and every one of them is a variety of monster. The invitations were very pretty. Little red hearts like valentine wishes painted on them. A heart is the most appropriate symbol for this occasion, as this party is being held in my house and I am Mr Loveheart. Curious symbol, the heart, isn't it? They are all over my clothes. They are all over the invitations. I even have my keyholes shaped as hearts. Every door opens a heart. What is my obsession with them really?

Sometimes I think I am quite mad.

Sometimes I think I am a strange key. Swallow me and I will unlock every door inside of you.

The stars this evening are really something special. The sky looks like it has been sliced open like a belly and they are all falling out. We are always half in another world, I suppose. When I look through my telescope I still keep an eye out for my father.

Dear Daddy, if only you had been made of stronger stuff. You're floating out there like a limp-winged angel. Not much help really. The planets tonight hang on wires like a theatre curtain. I just need to turn the wheel to make them move. We are all in some ways collectors of oddities. I happen to like stars and hearts. Mr Fingers, on the other hand, likes his clocks, tickety-tock.

We are having someone special for dinner tonight. She's in a cage hanging over the dining table. She's a lot bigger than she was before and she doesn't look very happy. Dearie me. The lace trim on my sleeves has fallen into the chocolate pudding, now that is a problem. You must always look your best for parties such as these. And you should see the dining hall, it looks splendid. Enough food for a hundred guests. A feast to feed a hundred demons in dinner suits. We all have big appetites and sharp teeth. And I am one of them.

A great mirror hangs in the dining room. Shall we look at our reflections? Am I the only one who doesn't want to look too closely? And what does that make me, a half monster? I look at them all, eyeing up the buffet, wanting to get started. Mr Fingers sits in my father's chair, seated like a king. While my real father is lost in space somewhere.

The woman – Mirror – stares at me from the cage. Drugged by the cowardly Dr Cherrytree. Her eyes are open, she is aware of everything going on. Something inside me wants to stroke her face, something inside me wants to save her, save myself. I wander over to the great table of food to be near her.

"Hello, Miss Mirror, how you've grown."

Mr Fingers rises from his chair to make his speech. "Welcome, friends." A hundred pairs of eyes turn to look at him. The woman, Mirror, sits slumped in the cage. I stand next to her, dressed in my bloodiest red. Daddy, the Demon Lord of the

Underworld, is speaking, so we must all be quiet and listen.

"Thank you so much for coming to my home," he preaches.

It is *my* home. It does not belong to him. I glance at Dr Cherrytree standing by his side. He continues, "Tonight, friends, we have a very special guest. You may have noticed a woman in a cage over the table," (and he laughs – oh, how funny he is!) "Well, she is our dinner. It has taken me quite a while to find her. She has moved from an Egyptian tomb to a grandfather clock to a little girl. And now here she is. And once she is eaten, I will absorb the soul of the Egyptian princess!" A round of applause.

Mr Fingers looks over to me. "And this would not have been possible without the help of my son, Loveheart."

Another round of applause. Why are they clapping? Why do I hear teacups breaking?

The drug inside her makes it hard for her to speak, but she tries. She looks through me like light through a diamond. Blinding me momentarily. What witchcraft is this? I can see my mother's face reflected on hers. I can feel my father's body frozen in space. All the noise around me, a hundred voices and yet it is her silence that is making me listen.

I was born a prince in a great kingdom. My mother and father were murdered by monsters. I was kidnapped and changed by a demon. My soul is a black hole. And yet she is making me want to kill every wicked thing in this house until a great pile of bodies is left with Mr Fingers on the top of the heap. I look at the dinner guests; child killers, rapists, fraudsters and they are inside my father's house, they are inside *my* house. I can hear her speaking to me. She is making me remember my name.

Loveheart   **Loveheart**
          Loveheart
Loveheart   *Loveheart*
     Loveheart   Loveheart
          Loveheart
          Loveheart
               Loveheart   Loveheart
     Loveheart   *Loveheart*

She reaches her hand through the cage and touches mine. "Mr Loveheart," she says with difficulty, "the lemon drizzle sponge is a little dry."

"Yes it is," I reply, and take my pistol out. There are tears running down my face.

I point it at Mr Fingers.

PART TWO

JULY 1888

The Clockmaker
TICK TOCK

My name is Alfred Chimes. I run a small clock-making and repair shop in East London, and I am seven hundred years old and not yet dead. The question then remains, how have I managed to prolong my life? The answer, I'm afraid, is not a pretty one. I am a killer of children. I stuff their souls into my clocks. Do you know what the soul of a child looks like? They are fairylights, little dazzling things. Zooming, sparkly and hopelessly scatty. Food for angels.

I make very fine clocks, for a very fine price. I suppose I am part serial killer, part magician. To the human eye, I look about eighty years old and I stoop and shuffle about. My beard is long and white. No one suspects what I really am. I am essentially overlooked. I am the wallpaper, always in the background.

Today I received a gift, wrapped in pink paper with hearts all over it. It was a handcrafted grandfather clock, one that I myself had made many years earlier. The message on the card read:

Thought you'd like it back. I fancied a clear out.
   Mr Loveheart 🍎

It had been battered about a bit and the soul was missing but it was still a very beautiful clock, good enough to lick all over.

I had previously sold it to his father, who had been a very good client of mine until his untimely disappearance. I had heard of his son, this notorious Mr Loveheart. Mad as a hatter, they said. An eccentric. Funny dress sense. Unlike his father who had seemed to me an introverted gentleman, with an obsession for time machines. Fell into one, so rumour had it. And now his son had contacted me. Curious fellow.

I wheeled the clock into the back room of my shop. With a little love I could bring it back to its former glory and sell it on at a nice price.

And then the doorbell rang and in stepped a policeman, very smartly dressed. Not at all the usual type. His face had strong features: a large nose and the most piercing hawkish eyes. Accompanying him was an officer of a lower rank, who fumbled with his jacket and didn't wipe his feet on the doormat.

"Good morning, sir. My name is Detective Sergeant Percival White and this is Constable Walnut. We are investigating a missing child case and have been making inquiries locally. Do you have a moment for some questions?" His voice was strong and steady. Incorruptible, I thought.

"Of course, sergeant. What would you like to know?" What an interesting day. A gift from an eccentric and a visit from the police.

"The girl's name is Daphne Withers, daughter of a local barrister. She went missing two days ago," and he showed me a photograph of her. Hair long and yellow, tied with a ribbon. I remembered her coming into my shop for a gift for her father. I remembered stuffing her into a barrel and throwing her into the Thames. Her essence was in a beautiful little wristwatch sitting in my window, a lady's watch with a topaz decoration of a butterfly.

"Hmm. I am afraid I have never seen the child."

Something changed in the expression of the detective. It was light moving through shadow.

"That's interesting."

"How so?" I inquired plainly.

"Her mother says she was coming to your shop to acquire a watch for her father as a present for his birthday."

"Well, I am rather old. I don't remember everything clearly much anymore."

Constable Walnut scribbled something down. I continued, "I suppose if she had been the daughter of a market trader, you wouldn't be making any inquiries."

Detective Sergeant White looked steely at me. "It is true that police resources are not always fairly distributed to every missing child case, but I make a point of investigating them all, sir."

"I am sure you are a credit to your superiors."

"Please take another look at her picture, Mr Chimes. Maybe it will jog your memory."

I examined the picture again. Clicked my tongue in a way I thought gave the impression of racking my old brain for a memory. It reminded me of her hair and the way it smelt lemony.

"No, I really can't recall her face."

"How long have you been in this shop, sir?"

"Oh, it must be fifty years. I really should retire, but I love my work so much."

"Do you have an assistant?"

"No, I work alone. I have a cat though," and I pointed

to the black lump of fur with the jade eyes which sat perched on the chair. "Her name is Cleopatra."

She was the only witness to my atrocities and she, I am sure, would remain silent on the matter.

"How's business?" asked Constable Walnut.

"Very good, thank you. I get a lot of requests for handmade pieces. Some of my clients live abroad and most of them are rich, with peculiar tastes. But I do get the odd person frequent my shop, though most around this area can't really afford my prices."

"Are you married, or have anyone staying with you?" inquired the detective.

"I am completely alone and I have sadly never married. I was never lucky enough to meet the right woman."

Detective Sergeant White looked eagle-eyed around the shop, and it was then that he spotted something. I realized I had made a mistake. Around Cleopatra's neck was a yellow ribbon, which I had taken off the girl, kept as a memento. He had spotted it. But it surely wasn't enough proof.

The detective examined the photograph of the girl and then stared at the cat. "Would you mind if we looked around the premises?"

So, he wasn't going to mention it. A ribbon wasn't enough to convict me.

"Of course. Through the door is my workshop and living quarters. Nothing much really."

And off the detective and his constable went. Cleopatra purred softly, I almost thought she was smirking.

A thick sea-green velvet curtain separated the shop from the workshop. It hung heavy, like a stage curtain. I followed them into the small space, the ladybird grandfather clock standing in the corner, my work desk covered in mechanisms and trinkets. The room was poorly lit but comfortable, and I watched Constable Walnut poke around while the detective merely viewed with his eyes. Sharp eyes, I thought. His attention was drawn to a pile of empty barrels and wooden crates in the corner of the room.

I explained them immediately. "For transportation of my large clocks."

And then his eyes moved to the ladybird grandfather clock.

"I've seen this before," he said. "From a previous case. A young girl was locked up inside it."

"I created the clock and sold it many years ago to Lord Loveheart."

"Lord Loveheart, who disappeared?" said Detective Sergeant White.

"Yes, his son, John Loveheart, returned it to me. I am not sure why. You may have heard of him, he's something of an eccentric."

"I would like a list of all of your clients, Mr Chimes."

I looked through my bureau drawers and retrieved a roll of my regular clients, which held about twenty or so names, and handed it to him begrudgingly. The list thankfully withheld the names of my more *sensitive* clients. He examined it carefully.

"Quite a collection of customers you have here. What makes your clocks so special?" And then he looked at me, and I felt for the first time in my life I had encountered someone who was able to see right through me. Eyes like a spiritualist. Telescopic.

"My work is very highly regarded. It's an artform, really. See the engravings on the clocks, delicate craftsmanship, it's hard to come by. I have been established for nearly fifty years so my reputation precedes me."

"And with a client list like this you choose to remain in this area of poverty and filth."

"It's my home, detective sergeant." And the children are easier to catch here, I thought.

The constable scribbled down everything I said

while the sergeant put the list of my clients into his pocket. "We may need to ask you further questions at a later date."

"Very well, but I am not sure how on Earth I can assist you. I have told you everything I know, which is nothing."

The detective stroked Cleopatra, who purred softly in response.

I watched them leave, the doorbell ringing as the door shut behind them. A delicate warning.

Along the Thames, a barrel bobbed up and down, a barrel that should have sunk to the bottom. It floated towards the shoreline.

II

Detective Sergeant White, Constable Walnut & the Clientele List

I had examined the list carefully as Constable Walnut and I walked back to the police station. "There's a lot of very influential people on this list, constable."

"You think he did it, sergeant?"

"He's either murdered her or sold her. The ribbon was the trophy. I want a full list of children that have gone missing in this area in the last year. He's made a mistake this time. She's a barrister's daughter."

"Yes, sir," Walnut replied.

"In the meantime, we shall be paying a visit to some of his clients."

I spent that afternoon gaining information on Mr Chimes' clientele list. Of the twenty names, fourteen were located abroad, one was in Scotland.

The remaining accessible names were:

Dr Edmund Cherrytree *– a psychoanalyst who*
     resided in London.
Lady Rosamund Clarence *– widower who resided in*
     London.
Elijah Whistle *– a painter of portraits to the aristocrats,*
     whose patron was Lady Clarence.
Obadiah Deadlock *– a notorious recluse, who resided*
     in London.
Lord Loveheart *who had disappeared, but his son*
     John had made contact with Albert Chimes and
     resided on the outskirts of London.

Letters had been sent ahead immediately
announcing our forthcoming arrival.

I had been trying to formulate a connection. My
immediate suspicion was that Albert Chimes was
providing these clients with children that he
kidnapped and was transporting them in wooden
boxes in the guise of clocks. I had worked on cases
before of child abduction for brothels and the sex
trade.

I thought of the grandfather clock in Mr Chimes'
shop. I remembered that case. I had been on the
scene when the little girl had been pulled out of the

clock, still alive. A grandfather gone mad had stuffed two little girls in a coffin under his bed. I remember thinking what sort of world I was living in where this would happen. I thought that would be the last time I saw that awful clock and here it was again, a terrible warning.

Constable Walnut entered the room rather clumsily and interrupted my thoughts. "Sir, I've got the information for you. Sorry, it took a while to go through all the missing person reports."

"What have you got?"

"In the last year, there have been over seventy missing children reported in the East End. I compared it to other areas, sir, and it's significantly higher. I made some inquiries on Albert Chimes. A lot of large deliveries leaving his shop every month. Large wooden crates."

"Large enough to put a child inside?"

"Yes, sir. Coffin sized."

We arrived in the early evening at the impressive and rather intimidating townhouse of Lady Clarence. I made Constable Walnut polish his boots before we left. Lady Clarence sat in the drawing room, wearing a lavish purple gown. Above her, an enormous painting hung, like a mirror, depicting her sitting on the same sofa in the same dress. The effect was unnerving to say the least. A mirror image. A doppelganger trapped in a painting. She was in her fifties with unusual almond shaped eyes and her teeth, which were clenched, were yellow. Sitting by her side, perched like a loyal dog, sat the artist, Elijah Whistle. He was an uncomfortably thin-looking gentleman with oiled black hair and a nervous disposition. His hands trembled slightly, gripping the sofa. I wondered how he could be steady with a paint brush.

"Lady Clarence and Mr Whistle." I'd taken off my hat. "Thank you for seeing us."

"I have to be at the opera in an hour, sergeant, so let's make this brief shall we?" she sneered. Her eyes fixed upon me, her doppelganger equally inhospitable.

"Of course. Could you tell me how you know the gentleman Albert Chimes, please?"

She didn't flinch and looked rather annoyed. "Albert Chimes is my clockmaker. I acquire specially designed time pieces from him." She held out her wrist. "Such as this."

I moved closer to her and looked at the wristwatch; it was made of silver and had a ring of little yellow flowers in a precious stone around the clock. It made a tiny humming sound, a delicate whirring.

"And how did you meet Albert Chimes?"

"I have never met Mr Chimes. My father used to obtain time pieces from him and I have simply continued to use him for special commissions."

I turned and looked at Mr Whistle. "And you, sir, you have also had pieces commissioned from Mr Chimes?"

Mr Whistle looked a little uncomfortable, his fingers tapping against his knee. "What's this about exactly, has he done something?"

"Please answer the question, sir."

"Lady Clarence recommended him to me when I needed a new pocket watch. But I have never met him."

"Are they expensive?"

"Very," said Lady Clarence proudly. "And worth every penny. He's an artist and unrivalled in Europe as a watchmaker."

"May I see your pocket watch, Mr Whistle?"

Mr Whistle passed it over to me, smoothing his hair back. It was silver with a soft whirring sound.

"It's very handsome," I said. "I wonder if you would look at this list and tell me if you are acquainted with any of the individuals on here?"

I passed the list to Lady Clarence first, who ran her eyes over it. "The Scottish duke, Campbell, I met at a hunting party a few years ago. Other than Elijah here, the only other person I had any acquaintance with was the former Lord Loveheart. His son John is a rogue and a wastrel, so I hear."

"And you, sir?" I said, passing the list to Elijah. His little dark eyes swept carefully over the names.

"I have heard of Obadiah Deadlock. He is a recluse and astronomer. I have also met Lord Loveheart's son, who came to an exhibition of my paintings at the Royal Academy. He was quite rude about my work."

"What did he say?"

"He said my art was whimsical tripe."

Constable Walnut coughed and scribbled down some hasty notes.

"Really?"

Lady Clarence responded, "Elijah is a superb portrait artist and has had many commissions. He was my discovery: I found him doing botanical illustrations for a reverend in Hove. I spotted his gift. Saved him from a life of near poverty in that accursed hole."

"Hove really isn't that bad. It's quite nice in the summer," remarked Constable Walnut.

"Thank you, Walnut," and I gave him a knowing glance to be quiet. I looked again at the portrait of

Lady Clarence. "It's very lifelike. When did you paint it?"

Elijah fumbled with his answer and looked to Lady Clarence, who replied, "Last summer."

Why would he be unsure of the date? I wondered.

"I am quite fond of still life myself, the odd bowl of fruit," Walnut persisted.

"Thank you, constable, I am sure no one is interested in your opinion of art."

"Will that be all then, sergeant?" She glared at me.

"One last question." I handed her the photograph. "Have you ever seen this girl before?"

Lady Clarence looked at the photograph. "She looks quite common. No, I haven't, who is she?"

I handed it to Elijah and he handed it back to me rapidly. "No."

"What is this all about, exactly, sergeant?" demanded Lady Clarence.

"The young girl has gone missing."

"And what has this got to do with us and Mr Albert Chimes?"

"We are just gathering information at present."

"But you obviously think there is a link," spoke Elijah, and as he said this he stroked his pocket watch. It was discreetly done but I was transfixed by this gesture. He stroked it almost adoringly, sexually even. I knew then they were involved somehow. But I still had no proof.

"We will leave you alone, to enjoy the opera," I said, and put my hat back on. The eyes of the portrait followed me out and the manservant shut the door rather abruptly behind us.

"What do you think, sir?" said Constable Walnut. "That painter's a funny bugger."

"They know what's happened to her."

We caught a cab to the residence of Obadiah Deadlock, who lived in a darker area of town, near a large cemetery. His home was quite shabby on the outside, and I knocked loudly on the door until a plump gentleman wearing a red velvet smoking jacket and a turban opened the door. He was ginger haired and his face was large, white and flabby.

"I've been expecting you," he said, and we entered into a very dimly lit room. The house itself was in disarray, wallpaper hanging off the walls, mouse droppings on the carpet. A stuffed cobra lying on the sofa and various charts and graphs of planets lay strewn about the floors. In an adjacent room an enormous telescope probed out into the night sky, the floor cluttered with empty plates of bits of food and I could hear mice squeaking and scurrying about. "How can I assist you, gentlemen?" He was at least polite.

"Do you know a gentleman named Albert Chimes?"

"I do not know him personally, but I acquire my clocks through him. He came very highly recommended to me a few years ago."

"Who recommended him to you?"

"My brother, Nathaniel, who lives in India."

"He's on the list, sergeant," Constable Walnut added.

"List?" Obadiah said.

"A list of clients of Mr Chimes. Please take a look at it and tell me if you know any of them."

Mr Deadlock's podgy hands gripped the piece of paper. "Apart from my brother, I only know of Mr Loveheart, although I have never met him. I do not socialize. I am a recluse, dedicated to my life's work."

"Which is?"

"The study of the solar system, the planet alignments, the stars. I have written many papers on the matter, all published."

"May I see your clock?" I asked, and pointed to the mantelpiece where a golden clock sat with a constellation design and the same soft whirring.

"What makes his clocks so special?" I asked.

At this, Mr Deadlock looked a little surprised. "They are unique."

"In what way, exactly?"

He was quite uncomfortable with this question and hurriedly answered, "The craftsmanship, of course."

I held out the picture of the missing girl. "Have you ever seen her before?"

"As I have said, I see no one. You are my first visitors for months, excluding delivery men."

"Your telescope is very impressive."

"Thank you. I suppose I am a voyeur of the cosmos." He chuckled to himself.

Walnut scribbled that comment down, scratching his head, not sure what it meant. My eyes were searching over Obadiah's constellation maps. Some of them looked hundreds of years old, beautifully hand drawn, yellowish paper curling at the edges. Fragmenting. The clock chimed, the cogs in my brain turned, and I said the word, "Time."

"Excuse me?" replied Obadiah.

"Eight-thirty," said Walnut.

"It's a metaphor, you stupid turnip!" cried Obadiah.

I thanked him for his time and left him in the soft darkness, with only the ticking whir of his clock for company.

Our last visit of the evening was to the Loveheart house on the edge of London. In the carriage Constable Walnut ate his sandwiches. Cheese and pickle. Constable Walnut's greatest joy in life was food.

We were driving through the estate of Loveheart, which was magnificent. It really was something out of a fairy tale. The drive towards the house was covered in great trees which stretched and twisted, and a carpet of wildflowers lined the path. I could for a moment imagine a prince on a white horse galloping through this landscape, it was so dreamlike.

"This Loveheart chap," said Constable Walnut, with a mouthful of food. "They say he's a bit off his head."

Our carriage pulled up in front of the house, which was white and enormous. We were welcomed by a butler who led us into a hallway, where a spiral staircase coiled to the heavens, with a violent red carpet dotted with hearts. Mr Loveheart greeted us as he descended the staircase, wearing electric blue velvet with heart shapes embroidered on his waistcoat, and his hair was the most shocking colour of yellow. Constable Walnut leaned toward me. "If he wore that down the East End he'd get knifed pretty quickly."

"Good evening, gentlemen," said Mr Loveheart. His voice had a soft, supernatural quality to it. He was really quite strange to look at, but fascinating.

"Good evening, Mr Loveheart. I am–"

"I know who you both are. How can I assist you in your inquiries?"

"You recently sent a grandfather clock to Mr Albert Chimes, the clockmaker. How do you know this man?"

"I do not know him. My father used his services. I returned one of his creations. I'm doing a spot of spring cleaning, getting rid of the clutter."

I handed him the client list. "Do you know any of these people, sir?"

Mr Loveheart took the list and read it, his eyes peeking up from the paper. "I know of them all. I have met only one of them – Elijah Whistle at the Royal Academy. He's a donkey of a painter, earns his money flattering the rich, painting them on thrones and such."

"He hasn't painted your picture then, sir?"

Mr Loveheart smiled generously. "I would rather stab myself with a fork that let him try that."

Constable Walnut scribbled down some notes, chuckling to himself.

I handed him the photograph of the girl. "Do you recognize her?"

"No. What has she got to do with Albert Chimes? Has he been a naughty boy and done something terrible to her?"

"Why, do you think he's capable of such a thing?" I said, staring at him.

"Have you seen his clocks? They are quite remarkable, rather special. My father knew him very well, did a great deal of business with him. He said he was quite a strange man. Unusual people, in my experience, tend to have unusual hobbies."

"What are you suggesting, Mr Loveheart?"

"I'm not *suggesting* anything, I am telling you that in my opinion he probably killed her, and many other children too."

"Do you have proof?"

"No, sadly, but have you asked your list of clients why his clocks are so special? Why they would pay a small fortune to have one?"

"Tell me why," I demanded.

Mr Loveheart sighed. "I am not going to do your

job for you, sergeant."

"Then stop wasting my time. I cannot arrest a man without evidence. If you know something, tell me. A young girl's life may be in danger."

Mr Loveheart was quite taken aback for a moment, and then laughed. "Oh, you're getting cross with me. I have no evidence. You must find that. As for the girl, I think you are too late."

"Mr Loveheart! Enough of this nonsense." I was furious with him. "Give me proof so I can arrest this villain"

"I will give you some advice, Detective Sergeant White," Loveheart said with a dark seriousness. "Don't arrest him. Kill him."

"I'm not a vigilante."

"It will never go trial. He'll never swing for it. Dearie me. Are you out of your depth, sergeant?" He examined me whimsically. "Yes, you are, aren't you. You're a clever chap but you do need assistance with this one. So, let me help you a little. The client list you hold in your hands – *they are all involved.* Including my late father. But I am not. Who have you got left to visit?"

"In the morning we are going to question Dr Edmund Cherrytree."

"Ahh, the psychoanalyst. He's a nasty piece of

work. Look at his photographs when you are there, sergeant. Especially the ones in his office. Look carefully."

"He's wasting our time, sergeant," noted Constable Walnut. "I think he's been on the sherry and possibly the laudanum."

"Shut up, Walnut. Mr Loveheart, stop playing games with me, just tell me what you know."

"Just look at the photographs, sergeant. You need to see for yourself. You are entering into something very unusual. Also, I wouldn't be surprised if Lady Clarence has hired someone by now to get rid of you."

"Why are you telling me any of this?"

"Because I don't care about these people. They are monsters. And I know a great deal about monsters. Maybe I want to see a happy ending. Maybe I have seen too much horror myself. I believe you have. You know where to find me if you have any other questions. I take it you can see yourselves out." He gestured at the door.

"Wait," I said.

"Yes?' replied Mr Loveheart curiously.

"What is happening to the children? I must know."

Mr Loveheart looked a little sad, then

straightened his lacy cuff. "He's putting them inside the clocks, sergeant." And off he walked, grinning like a schoolboy, and left us standing there for a moment, dumbfounded.

As the carriage pulled up outside the headquarters, Constable Walnut stretched out his legs. "Well, it's been a long night. I could do with a pint."

There was a commotion and an officer ran up to us. "Sergeant, a body's been found sir, near Tower Bridge."

There, the barrel had been washed up against the shore, broken and stinking of something rotting. A small, pale arm hung out of it. A couple of policemen pulled the body of Daphne Withers out.

I'd seen a barrel just like it, in the clockmaker's cellar.

July 1888
MR LOVEHEART VISITS
ALBERT CHIMES

It was terribly smelly in that part of London. I knocked on the shop door of the clockmaker and waited for him to answer. *Rat a tat tat.* The door creaked open and we stared at one another.

"Hello, Albert. I am John Loveheart, and you have been a very bad boy."

He let me in, the silly fish – they always do. He lit an oil lamp and we stood in his little curious shop. His pale eyes watched me carefully. "Why are you here?"

"Well, I'm not shopping for clocks. I'm really not interested in extending my life unnaturally. My life is already far too unnatural. I am a little surprised that a wealthy alchemist like yourself would be living in a shit pit."

He didn't reply.

"But," I continued, "I was curious to meet a man so prominent a part in my father's life. You fuelled his addiction with your little time contraptions. He never had much time for me as a child."

Mr Chimes replied, "So your daddy didn't love you enough. Well maybe you weren't very lovable. It's late and I'm tired, what have you come here for?"

"And so you should be tired. I would be too if I were hundreds of years old. Why is it you people are obsessed with living so long on this Earth? Please tell me. I would love to know."

"You wouldn't understand. Now get out of my shop."

"Oh you really are no fun at all. And that detective is so close to catching you. I suppose your little time machines don't bode too well against the hangman."

"I can disappear easily enough. I am seven hundred years old. I have killed thousands and thousands of..."

I pulled out my little silver pistol and shot him in the head. "Blah blah blah. You're boring me."

A black cat with jewel-like eyes watched me from the cabinet, yawning. I picked her up to take her home with me. I thought the ribbon round her neck was quite charming.

When I stepped into the street, a small boy was staring at me.

"Mr Loveheart?' he said.

"*Yes?*" I replied, stroking the cat, "And you are?"

"Death."

"*Ah, I see.*" I was intrigued.

"I have been watching you with interest, Mr Loveheart."

"I suppose I *am* interesting. Is there anything I can help you with? Directions perhaps? Are you lost?"

"Are you an angel or a devil?" and his voice sent ripples of electricity through the night air.

"I haven't decided yet." And I wandered off down the grim little alley, whistling.

IV

I arrived at the asylum at exactly a quarter past two. A row of fat pigeons sat on the wall, overlooking my arrival, suspiciously. The gates were spiked iron, both gloomy and menacing, encircling the building like the tail of a great dragon, the paving stones underneath wet with a slime trail. The warden's name was Fuggle and he had wooden teeth, something I hadn't seen for quite a while. It amused me.

I introduced myself. "Doctor Edmund Cherrytree. I've come to see Ernest Merryworth."

The warden looked me up and down. "Oh, the doctor. You're doing a study. I remember your letter."

"Yes, I have come to examine his behaviour. I am writing a book on the criminally insane."

Fuggle laughed, his wooden teeth slipping about. "You've come to the right place." He escorted me down a deep, long, white corridor, jingling his keys by his side. "He's been as good as gold, doctor, since he got the bad news."

"Bad news?"

"He's dying. Got a month or so left. Something wrong with his heart." And Fuggle laughed.

"What's so amusing?"

"His heart. Of course there's something wrong with it. He's a bad sort. You know what he did to his granddaughters." Fuggle looked at me sideways and continued, "Killed two of them and stuffed the other one in a clock."

"Man is capable of redemption, Mr Fuggle."

Mr Fuggle taps his nose. "I've seen it all. The very worst of man. Angels can forgive him, Doctor Cherrytree. I won't."

We arrived outside the cell of Mr Merryworth. Mr Fuggle opened the door with a little key. Ernest sat by the window reading, and he turned towards me, so I could see the front cover of the book. It was about clock making.

Fuggle coughed into his hand. "Well, I will leave you both to it. I will be outside if you need anything. Just shout."

"Thank you," I said, and stared over at Ernest. "I believe you have been expecting me?"

"I got your letter." His voice was croaky. He was a withered old man. His cell had a small bed and a chamber pot, a desk and chair. The only other item in the room was the book in his hands. "I'm dying."

"Yes, I'm aware, and I may be able to help you with that. For a price."

"What do you want?"

"I need to know where your granddaughter is. The one who survived. The one you locked in the clock. If you tell me this I can extend your life."

Ernest put the book down. "That's a very tempting offer. And why is my granddaughter so important to you, eh? Do you like little girls, doctor? Do you like to play with them?"

"No. But you certainly do. Where is she?"

"A policeman took her. Adopted her. The last I heard they had gone to Cairo."

"What is this policeman's name?"

"Goliath Honey-Flower. He's Egyptian. Huge bugger. He saved her. Pulled her out of the clock."

"Thank you."

"And now will you help me? Will you give me more time, doctor?" and he rested his hand on the book.

"I will send you something in the post, Ernest. You will live."

"Before you go, tell me what happened to my clock?"

"It never belonged to you. You stole it and it was returned to your employer."

Ernest looked very sad for a moment. "I loved it. It was the only thing I have ever loved."

And I left him with his sadness, strange mutterings, and his book on clock making.

It had started to rain when I left Fuggle and his pigeons and walked out of the gates of the asylum. I thought about grandfathers, granddaughters and grandfather clocks. *Tickety-tock.* The rain fell like seconds and time was laughing, gently. I examined my pocket watch, which had a serpent with ruby eyes. It was soft magic within my hands. I had acquired the watch from Albert Chimes the clock maker. He had told me that inside my watch was the soul of a baby. And I had been so pleased, so very pleased.

July 1888

I suppose at some point I was going to get caught. It was the heat of summer when he arrived. The detective with hawk-eyes.

He was waiting for me in the lobby with his constable. They introduced themselves as White and Walnut, investigating the case of a missing girl and a possible link to the clockmaker Albert Chimes. I was handed a picture of the girl and a client list of Mr Chimes, both of which I examined with unease. "Well, detective sergeant, I don't recognize the young girl and I am not acquainted with anyone on this list."

The detective had a very odd expression on his face. "Last night Daphne Withers' body was found in a barrel floating along the Thames. This morning the body of Albert Chimes was found in his shop. He had been shot in the head."

Constable Walnut intervened, "And his cat has gone missing."

"Oh dear," I said, "I am not really sure I can help you."

"Can you account for your whereabouts last night, doctor?" The detective had the stare of a mesmerist about him. Deep, like whirlpools.

"Yes. I was here with my assistant, Peter. We were reviewing some of my patient cases and having a late supper."

Constable Walnut raised an eyebrow.

"Is Peter about to confirm your alibi?"

"No," I said, and I could see Constable Walnut was very amused with himself. "He will be back later today. I will get him to make a statement at the police station."

"Thank you. I wonder if you could tell me about the photographs on the walls. If you could explain to me exactly what they are."

"What do they have to do with your inquiries?"

"I am interested in the individuals who were clients of Albert Chimes. You were one of those clients. And your photographs interest me."

"Very well. They are spiritualist photographs. They depict the moment the soul leaves the body."

"How did you acquire them?"

"I am a photographer. I have travelled a great deal in my past. I witnessed some terrible accidents and deaths."

"And you took pictures while people were dying?" the Detective stared at me. That gaze again. It reminded me of a mirror.

"How exactly do I answer that, detective? Hmm? I couldn't save these people."

"You didn't try."

"Are you going to arrest me for photographing the human soul?"

"I would like to see inside your office," he said. And I let him in. He was interested in two pictures and a photograph that hung on the wall. The largest painting above my desk was a watercolour of a Norfolk view, a white sail boat drifting lazily along the river. Near the window, the detective then examined another smaller watercolour of a dragonfly trapped in a jam jar. "Who painted these?" he inquired.

"I did. I was rather an amateur artist and photographer before I studied psychoanalysis. Sometimes I feel as though I have had two lives," and I instinctively touched my watch. For a moment I thought he saw this gesture and looked at me curiously.

He moved over towards the photograph behind the door. And he stood there for some time, examining it, then he plucked it off the wall.

"Tell me," he said, "about this photograph."

"It's a picture of me with Albert Chimes in Paris. We are standing on a bridge."

"Tell me about your relationship with him."

"I met him twenty years ago, in Paris. That picture was taken shortly after we met. He had an exhibition of his clocks in a small gallery. They were beautiful things."

Detective Sergeant White held the photograph in his hands like a holy object.

"Is there something wrong, detective?"

"Yes," he said softly. "There is something wrong with this picture. You say this was taken twenty years ago and yet neither of you have aged. How is that possible?"

"I really don't understand what you're trying to insinuate. You are accusing me of not aging. Are you going to arrest me for it?" and I laughed.

Detective Sergeant White looked very seriously at me. "I believe that somehow these clocks are extending your lives. Children are being murdered and you are involved."

I sat myself down on the sofa intended for my

patients. "You can prove absolutely nothing. And you have now placed yourself in a very dangerous position."

Detective Sergeant White placed the photograph on the desk and left with his constable. I put the photograph back on the wall and brushed the dust off. Albert Chimes smiled back at me, that wicked old alchemist.

October 1887
MIRROR IN EGYPT

When Goliath rescued me from the clock and lifted me deep within his arms, I remember closing my eyes, keeping them shut. Soft darkness in my head, pounding, fizzing pressure. A sheep's head boiling in the pot. For the light was burning my eyes; like grandfather striking matches to ignite his tobacco pipe, gripped by his great fingers, those dirty sausages. The flame, a phosphorous green glow with something alien underneath. He spat on the flame to put it out.

That's what you do with fire –

    put
    it
    out.

Goliath had lifted me out of the clock, my coffin. An alien whiff surrounding me, as the hinges creaked open. I had been swimming, I had been drowning, I had been with the dead, talking with ghosts. But he carried me away, far away. My eyes shut tight. To Egypt, to Egypt.

I was holding his hand, under a sun that looked like a lemon floating in the sky.

"Why is it so bright?" I said, peering squinty eyed.

Goliath squeezed my hand. "To sizzle up the demons."

We were standing outside a lopsided wooden bookshop in Cairo. It was painted orange and pink with little balconies and pot plants with creeping greenish fingers. Goliath showed me around Cairo while we were staying with his father, the archaeologist: he is a man who digs up the dead and finds secret things.

I know I am supposed to be with Goliath. I am sewn into him, the threads in my tummy criss-crossed with his. If you cut us apart we fall to pieces.

In the street was a man with a donkey, the saddlebags loaded up with books for delivery. I patted the donkey's nose. He smelt of earthy things and warm fuzzy fur. Wet tongue, black flies buzz like wicked angels around his eyes. I slapped them away. We walked onwards down the street, the air smelling of sweet-shit and honey. A sort of fairy stench. I liked the smell of this place, I liked the feel of Goliath's great hand and its black fuzz of hair. He held me so tight, a bearish grip. That is what safety feels like. Safety is a great bear standing beside you.

always
a wall of muscle
a great row of teeth.

I would think, *If you touch me again, Grandfather, he will crush you with his great paws. Chomp on your bones. Lick your blood from his fur. Leave no trace of you.*

We passed a café where men were sitting smoking tobacco with their snake pipes. They watched us pass, I think the colour of my hair caught their eyes. Grandpa always said my hair was too red. The Devil likes red, he said. The Devil likes red and little girls.

"They are staring at me," I said.

Goliath rubbed my head with his great hand, so my hair would stick up. "Because you look like a little fire imp," and then he picked me up into his arms and carried me onto his shoulders. I got a whiff of the tobacco and its hot, smoky beetle-scent. I waved at the pipe smokers, who wore long white nightshirts, as though sleepy and ready for bed. I thought, I am a fire imp. I am a fire imp. I am fire.

And someone will try to put me out.

I reached upwards towards the lemon floating in the sky. I saw boys sewing a tent with ripples of colour like peacock eyes: dazzling emerald and deep-sea blues, and they were smiling and laughing. Goliath pointed to the university – its entrance carved in leaf-like patterns. A student sat on the steps, putting on his slipper-like shoe. There was a hole in it and his toe was sticking out. We continued along the streets of Cairo, hot and yellow, burnt. White donkeys with cargo, bright birds in wicker cages, moon symbols on doors and onion shaped towers reaching into the sky like telescopes. I wondered if there were princesses in the towers? Hair like a cloth of gold? But the princesses in Egypt would have hair as black as nightfall. Black as a theatre curtain closing. Black as an ending.

I saw the heads of men up here, little white caps and coloured turbans. Heads floating towards a blue Mosque. Star shapes imprinted on the walls. A temple of the night sky. I reached out and touched the magic shapes with my hands. Lay a hand on a star surface. An imprint.

"Do they worship the stars?" I asked Goliath.

"Yes. They believe when we die, we return to the stars," he replied, and handed me some figs which I gobbled up. I tried to count the stars on the temple, but I ran out of numbers in my head and the stars took over. Head full of them, we walked on.

Two old men were bent over a game of draughts; I saw them move their pieces. Old knobbly fingers, white beards, missing teeth. A piss pot rested by the entrance to their home, freshly emptied. Onwards we walked, and I saw a great white bird fly overhead. Soaring. Its wings were made of angel pieces.

That is freedom. That is what freedom is.

1887
THE UNDERWORLD

Did I tell you that Daddy was dead? Yes, I think I did. He's floating in space, somewhere. Space, that heavy spooky hole of stars. I remember the night before Mr Fingers came to our house, I looked up into the dark sky at all that glitter, at all that wonderland of emptiness and I wanted to be sucked into it. And I suppose, in some ways I got my wish.

I remember watching Mr Fingers stuff my father into the black obsidian Egyptian sarcophagus in the hall. He wanted my father to tell him where the grandfather clock was, the clock that was stolen. My father was crying – he had no idea. And then Mr Fingers shut the lid and my father disappeared like a magician's assistant.

Goodbye, Daddy.

Mr Fingers, the man with the black spectacles and

the waistcoat dancing with ladybirds. Some sort of magic man. Some sort of demon. Some sort of father. And he took me by the hand and we walked outside in the snow. Everything was so white, as soft as sugar dusting. Hand in hand through the garden we walked, our footsteps squelching into the fuzzy snow.

"Where are we going?" I asked. And he smiled, a smile of a thousand cats. A smile of angels. A smile of sharks. Ice cool. Devil hot.

A spiral staircase appeared in the earth and down, down, down we stepped into the Underworld. The layers of earth were moulded into human faces, whose eyes, bulging and swollen, watched us descend. Souls trapped in the mud. Some glittery and green, others with eyes like leaves. Green beetles burrowed into their eye sockets and laid eggs in their mouths. I wanted to touch them with my finger but Mr Fingers kept hold of my hand and we continued down into the wet darkness.

In the Underworld a black river coils like a serpent around the palace of the King of the Dead. It bubbles and shimmers and I imagine there are strange creatures underneath with black scissor teeth and eyes swelling like pearls. The palace of Mr Fingers is enormous and filled with clocks that chime every quarter of an hour. There are odd shaped rooms and strange carvings. It is like a museum or mausoleum, stuffed with oddities. He squeezed my hand. "You are now a prince of the Underworld. This is your playground," he said, like any proud father. He is a kind of magician. He is a kind of madness.

My bedroom was in one of the towers. It was painted with stars and the cosmos. A great telescope peered out of the window like an enormous eye. I peered through it. What do the stars in the Underworld look like, I wondered? They seemed smaller, further away. Tiny dots of starlight, winking like fairy tale frog eyes. I am in the Land of the Dead. This is how the dead see the stars, at a greater distance. And this made me feel a great sadness.

I was in a great empty space. I was a prince of a great empty space. My room had a bookshelf stuffed with books, again, all on the stars and the planets. I sat on my bed and flicked through the pages of star charts and sketches of constellations. I held in my hands maps of the universe and yet I could only peer into them. Like my father, I had been placed in a tomb and I had disappeared.

I sat with my new father at the dinner table. My black-eyed Daddy. The clocks ticked round us.

"What is going to happen to me?" I asked him.

Mr Fingers peered over at me. "You will grow up here as my son."

"Why do you want the grandfather clock?"

"It has something inside of it."

"What?"

"Something I want."

"How will you find it?"

"I have my spies. My little blackbirds on the Earth with their beady eyes. Now eat your supper."

And so I ate. I gobbled down what was on my plate. After dinner, Mr Fingers scratched his belly and yawned. He reminded me of a great crocodile. How bright his eyes looked. Like glistening ebony. Like black magic. Like a serial murderer.

After dinner, Mr Fingers took me by the hand and led me down a long black corridor. On the walls were paintings of human bodies piled upon one another in great heaps. They twisted and writhed like worms in a jar. I was sure they were actually moving.

"You are going to meet the other princes, now. Your brothers." And he opened the door at the end of the corridor.

We stepped into a great circular chamber where a series of glass coffins stood in a row. Each glass coffin had a little boy inside with eyes as black as midnight.

Mr Fingers put his finger to his lips. "Shhhhh, they are sleeping. You are number fourteen. My fourteenth prince and my favourite boy."

"My brothers," I whispered. I looked at them in their glass cages. Identical dolls. One of them was softly snoring and I could see, yes, I could see his teeth. Little and very pointy, like tiny blades. They were my brothers and they were something horrible. They had black hair and black eyes. My hair was yellow like my mother's, my eyes pale. I was not one of them. Mr Fingers put his hand on my shoulder.

"My dear boy. Tomorrow you can play with them. Now run off to bed and get some sleep."

And I ran. I ran into the tower and into my bedroom. I covered myself in star charts. I wanted to dream of the stars. I wanted to escape through my telescope, but I was in the Land of the Dead and my dreams were those of corpses.

In my dream I was in my old family home again. It was a place of charms and punishments. I was having dinner with my father and mother and Aunt Rosebud. We were eating something strange. We were eating an angel. It was still alive and its wings were beating like a heartbeat. I said, "I cannot eat this."

My father looked cross. "You must eat what you are told."

My mother said, "It's good for you. It will make you a strong boy."

My Aunt Rosebud added, "You have a weak brain. Angel meat will cure you."

I tried a piece of angel meat. Chewed it and swallowed. It tasted sweet. It tasted wrong. I spat it out and ran out of the room. My dead family watched me leave and continued eating. I ran out of the house and into the garden. I ran to the fields and to an old well at the bottom of the estate near the woods. I sucked my thumb by the well, and stroked the long grasses, touching the daisies. I peered down the well and saw Mr Fingers waving. "Jump down, little boy. Come with me."

I didn't want to eat angel meat. I didn't want to jump down the well. I had nowhere else to go. I saw the lake and started to run to it. It was big and cool and blue like suicide. I jumped in and sank to the bottom. I was safe there with the mermaids. I was drowning and safe.

When I woke up Mr Fingers was standing over me. He wanted me to meet my brothers. He wanted to tell us a story. We sat round our father like choirboys round a priest and he opened a big black book and began:

Once upon a time there were fourteen princes. And they lived in a magical kingdom deep down in the underworld. Their father was a very powerful magician and he was very proud of his boys.

Prince number 1 liked to carve faces in potatoes to make him laugh.

Prince number 2 liked to set fire to butterflies.

Prince number 3 liked girls with big hairy legs.

Prince number 4 liked to eat pancakes with sugar and butter.

Prince number 5 liked to chase ghosts and catch them in jars.

Prince number 6 liked to cut off heads and hang them from trees.

Prince number 7 liked to cut smiles into people's faces.

Prince number 8 liked to fall in love with mirrors.

Prince number 9 liked to draw strange symbols on doors.

Prince number 10 liked to tell pretty lies.

Prince number 11 liked to sit in graveyards.

Prince number 12 liked to steal love letters.

Prince number 13 liked to collect teeth.

Prince number 14 liked to stare at the stars.

And they were all so happy with their Daddy in the magical underworld. And they would do anything their Daddy would tell them. Anything.

Because if they ever disobeyed him, their Daddy would gobble them up in a heartbeat.

And he shut the book. I stared at my identical brothers with their black sharp eyes and wondered if it could get any worse.

A stupid question, really.

Prince Number 13

Number thirteen is supposed to be unlucky. Some people dispute this theory, saying it's superstitious nonsense. Well let me put everybody straight. Avoid number thirteen. It's the nastiest number there is.

Princes 1-12 were all alike. Daddy had made them himself with dark matter and his own juices. Sticky little identical creations. Voodoo doll eyes.

Prince Number Thirteen was different. He was like me.

Like me, he had a name. It was Tumbletee. Like me, he also had a hobby. He liked to collect teeth in little bags. Like me, Daddy had kidnapped him from the Earth to raise him in the Underworld. My brothers told me, "We are not allowed to play with him," and so I asked Daddy why not and he said:

"Because he is the game."

He slept in the black tower, near Daddy's chamber. Number Thirteen. One day I climbed the tower to visit him. I wanted to know the thirteenth prince. His bedroom overlooked the river of the dead, a ripple of black fleshy waters, a vinegar stink. Whereas my bedroom was covered in star maps, his room was dripping in blood, pooling like bright bursting flower heads around his feet. I noticed his skin was pitted and scarred and moony white. He was older than me and his eyes, knife-like, would slice through flesh. He had white hair, it was moonlight white. White as fairy dust.

"My name is Loveheart. I am your brother," I said.

He watched me intently, as through examining a bug. "Tumbletee. I like teeth. Let me see yours," and he moved closer to me and touched my incisors with his bloodied finger. "We are not like the others," he said. "You and I are different." His finger moved over my teeth, lover-like. I think he wanted to pull them out. I stared down at my feet. I was standing in red.

"Why is there so much blood?"

"Daddy says I am a supernova of cruelty. We are all monsters, little brother, but I am the worst of them," and he removed his finger from my mouth and shook my hand. I gripped his palm. It was icy, alien. Something deep inside me was screaming.

Kill him.
     Push
         him
              from the tower.

He smelt of spermy things. He knows what I am thinking, he knows. "Little brother," he said, "Little brother, I want so much for you to try to kill me."

I backed away from him, blood trailing on my feet. Marking my exit.

October 1887
EXCAVATION SITE OF THE
EGYPTIAN PRINCESS

Lemon hot. We boiled under the Cairo sun. Goliath brought me to the tomb of the princess, his father's excavation. The tomb entrance had been uncovered; I stepped closer, touched the walls with my fingers.

It fizzled cool magic.

Hieroglyphics. That is what Goliath calls them. To me they are a magic language. My finger outlined a feather shape, a wriggly snail, a bird. Each one has meaning, each one a word that forms a spell.

Above the entrance to the tomb in colours of black and gold there was a dazzling painting of a man with the head of a black dog. A jackal prince. I stroked his head. Imagined him on a lead in Hyde Park.

He looked part wicked to me, part of an under-world. I wondered what that would be like; would

177

there be a black river stuffed with souls? Would there be a sphinx asking a riddle I had no answer to? Would they cut out my tongue, write symbols on the walls with it. Make a marking of me; squeeze me into their alphabet?

Goliath lifted me up so I could see the patterns on the ceiling, "Can you see, little one, can you see the magic bugs?"

I could, I could see them crawling over the entrance to her death chamber. Red splodges. Tiny things. A hundred of them; they nibbled the sandstone, eating the structure. They formed spirals, turning in on themselves. Making circles of everything.

He carried me out of the magic space and I sat on his lap and ate honeycakes; licked my fingers and pointed to the top of the pyramids. What are they aiming at? Pinpointing a star?

So much yellow sand – under our feet and miles away. Spread like butter. The heat melts everything, turns me into goo.

The workmen had already found pieces of pottery near the entrance; shards painted green with white vampire fang shapes. The teeth of a crocodile maybe? I played with them in the sand; tried to make a jigsaw puzzle of them. Moved the pieces around. The picture remained unclear.

Men with shovels and carts moved across the sand; under shaded tents they played cards and drank coffee. Their hands were lined deep; cracks in paper. I waved at them; one of them waved back, his mouth a red hole with two wonky teeth.

"One day," Goliath said, "You will see inside the princess's tomb. See her sarcophagus. My father says she was a sorceress."

I squeezed his nose with my hand and laughed. "Did she have a big nose like you?" and I cuddled him. Squeezed him with love.

Together we walked across the sands hand in hand. The land was marked out, divided with excavation digs. The Pyramids of the Kings surrounded us as though we were pieces on a board game. We moved through the squares. Watched our footing.

The Game
TUMBLETEE & LOVEHEART

And so I grew up in the Underworld. There was no sense of time down there. The Underworld clocks *tick tocked* and Daddy gobbled the seconds up. Tumbletee told me Daddy had sent him many times to the Earth to do things for him. He had been to Egypt and seen the tombs of the Pharaohs, and he had walked the streets of Paris and been to gentlemen's clubs and danced with girls dressed in peacock feathers. Daddy said I was not ready to go to the Upperworld yet, but I was starting to change. My eyes, which were blue – the colour of my mother's – had become ink squid black. My big brother, Tumbletee, said I was unnaturally beautiful. He liked unnatural things.

Daddy said, "You have the face of an angel, Loveheart. You have a face that will break hearts."

I don't understand beauty. I looked at Tumbletee's face, it had pox scars. Its texture looked like porridge. If I ran my finger over his face and felt its lumps, would I feel ugliness? His face was a weird painting, a landscape of the moon. Craters and pits. I saw the galactic in him, the alien, the deep unknown.

Growing up in the underworld was like sinking into a deep well, black waters. I was losing myself, forgetting my name.

Loveheart   Loveheart

Loveheart

Loveheart   **Loveheart**

Loveheart   Loveheart

Loveheart

Loveheart

Loveheart

Loveheart

Loveheart

Loveheart

Love   love   love   love   love

heart

heart

heart

At meal times we sat round the dinner table with our Daddy. All fourteen princes. Row upon row of wicked black eyes. We were eating a giant blood pie. Daddy cut the slices, oozing so much red.

"Eat up, my sons," he said. "My wonderful boys."

I ate the blood pie, chewed on it. Gobbled it down. I was growing into a big, strong boy. I was eating something I shouldn't. It was poisoning me. I looked round the table at my brothers and I thought, I am the odd one out. The blood trickled down my throat, deep into my stomach. The more I ate Daddy's food, the more I was changing, my insides turning to black ooze.

I could hear the tick tock of Daddy's clocks – their constant noise. It filled my ears, drowned out other sounds. It was making me mad. He was making me mad. My mouth was full of blood, my head full of demented clocks. Year upon year. Year upon year. Layers of a trifle. I was the red jelly at the bottom, see me wobble.

Wobble on the plate

wobble

I remember my seventeenth birthday in the Underworld. Daddy was so proud of me. I was his favourite. Head full of fairies. Demented.

They called me Loveheart.

My big brother, Tumbletee, was taking me to the Upperworld. We were going to play a game. Wasn't that nice? I was very fond of games. Tumbletee told me I had an ancestral home and vast estate. Apparently I am the richest man in England, isn't that marvellous! If I played the game well, Daddy said I could go back to my castle and live in the Upperworld. I was wearing a lovely coat with red lovehearts over it. Daddy gave it to me as a present. I do like hearts, such a curious thing, the heart, and very tasty.

"What game are we going to play, brother?" I asked him.

Tumbletee put on his black top hat with a red sash, his white hair sticking out like silver threads, his voice a lizard hiss. "Follow me and you will find out, little brother."

August 1887

I returned the same day I was taken. Snow rested on the ground. Mad weather for August. Everything was topsy turvy. Dangling on all the trees around my ancestral home were severed heads hanging from the branches, dripping blood onto the snow.

"Do you like my gift?" Tumbletee licked his lips.

There must have been a hundred heads or more. Mad fruit.

"Yes, yes. We are in the thick of it. Deep like custard," and my big brother put his arm around me. "Before I leave you, you must do something for Daddy," and he guided me towards the front door of my white home. A head hung from the doorknocker, its eyeballs wobbling about like jelly. He opened the door with a great silver key. Sitting at the hall table was my mother.

"I dug her up for you," he joked.

The table was laid with a white lace teacloth and on it a pile of jam sandwiches and a steaming pot of tea. "Isn't this a warming reunion? Tea with Mother." And he guided me to a seat next to her. Her skin was green, her eyes clouded over. Mother. I remember you. I am a cracked teapot. The fault lines run deep. I could smell the rottenness of her. Tumbletee poured the tea and passed me the sandwiches. "Tuck in."

Isn't this a strange world? I am having tea with the dead. I am made of marmalade. I am smiling and smiling and cracking and breaking within your hands.

Dearie me, I dropped my teacup.

And he left me there. In my ancestral home with my dead mother and my vast gardens of chopped heads.

Madness is only a word.

Loveheart.

It was lying on my desk when I returned from Doctor Cherrytree's practice: a little white envelope with a loveheart ink splodge. A dangerous little thing.

Dear Detective Sergeant White,

You have been invited — Yes, you! — to an art exhibition of Elijah Whistle. All your favourite monsters will be attending.
Bring Walnut if you wish.

Mr Loveheart 🐍

"Constable Walnut!" I shouted, and he appeared, poking his head round the door.

"Yes sir?"

"It appears Mr Loveheart has decided to give us a helping hand."

The Moonstone Opera house, nestled near the Thames, was the venue for the evening art exhibition. It was raining heavily and the streets were oozing with liquid. Purple banners hung, heavy with rain, outside the doors and a soft velvet rope sealed the doorway. It was guarded by an attendant with white gloves, holding a large black umbrella.

"Very posh," sighed Constable Walnut. "I've often considered trying my hand at painting. Bit of an artistic gift running in my family," and he held up his hands. "Creative hands."

"I'd keep that to yourself, Walnut, if I were you."

We approached the attendant.

"Evening, gentlemen, may I see your invitations?" He glanced a somewhat suspicious eye over our invite and then reluctantly held the velvet rope aside. The building inside was circular, with a large selection of paintings adorning the walls.

We deposited our coats and stepped into the main exhibition area, in which twenty or so people were gathered. Above the main room was a high balcony overlooking the main exhibition, where an enormous painting of Lady Clarence was hung. She was lying, lizard-like, on a sofa in a vibrant maroon dress. Her expression was odd: it was a mixture of conceit and a strange slyness. And then I realized why, for her hand was resting on a clock. A secret message for all those involved, I thought. Suggesting she has some sort of power over death.

"It's quite a statement," a voice like little bells said next to me, and I turned and looked directly at Mr Loveheart. He was dressed in otherworldly green with red hearts bursting like stab wounds all over him. "Of course," he continued, "these people are all rather stupid. We must not be too hard on them. Their little magic clocks have made them a bit mad."

"Why exactly did you invite me here tonight, Mr Loveheart?"

"My life is a little dull at the moment, and I do like interesting scenarios. Spice things up a bit. Put you in the lion's den. See if anyone bites."

"How thoughtful of you," I said dryly.

"My pleasure. The art is dreadful and the guests are all dead. Look at them all, detective. Take a good look. You are in the underworld sipping champagne with corpses." And his eyes were bright with electricity.

I followed his gaze to the centre of the room,

where Elijah Whistle was standing next to Lady Clarence, both with a glass of champagne in their hands. He looked like a pussycat, as though she had been feeding him cream.

"Dead as doornails, the whole lot of them."

We moved softly round the edges of the exhibition and stood by a small series of oil paintings of human hands. Constable Walnut examined them, glancing down at his own. Comparing.

"Of course, you can't arrest anyone," sighed Loveheart.

"I could arrest you for killing Albert Chimes."

"I've done you a service, detective. I have avenged the death of Daphne Withers. And where will they get their pretty watches from now? I've put some pressure on them. Shaken them up a bit."

"I wanted Albert Chimes arrested. I nearly had enough evidence."

"They would have got him out." Loveheart looked out into the crowd. "They would have stopped you. I have saved your life."

"Do they know you killed him?"

"They think I'm a half-wit."

"And what are you really, Mr Loveheart?" I looked directly at him. He was surprised by the question and, I thought, rather saddened by it.

"I am," he said very softly, "rather dangerous...
"He turned and walked off towards the balcony.

Constable Walnut and I moved down a side corridor, where a row of miniatures of Elijah's early works were hung. They were botanical illustrations in black ink, dotted about like formula. I found them far more interesting than his portraiture. This was his work before he died. Before he met Lady Clarence. Before he was given his first demonic watch. This was who he had been. The illustrations were precise and methodical with sharp edges and a scientific line to them: they were curious dark little things. Ferns, mushrooms and weed-like creatures coiled over the wall, each with its scientific name, each with its own darkness.

"I don't like them. They give me the creeps," said Walnut, scratching his chin.

I could hear a splattering of applause and laughter behind us. Lady Clarence was giving a toast, her champagne glass lifted into the air, the crowd responding appropriately. The dead toasted the dead. All very civil. And then I saw Mr Loveheart walking towards the centre of the room, clapping in a long, slow motion. The crowd turned to watch him and parted for him like waves, lapping round his feet, circling him.

"Marvellous speech," cried Loveheart, "really splendid!"

"Walnut, follow me, something is about to happen." The constable and I edged closer to the main room.

Lady Clarence looked at Mr Loveheart rather pitifully. "Oh, John. It's lovely for us to finally meet. It's a shame your father can't be here. He was a wonderful man."

She was mocking him. A smile like a pair of scissors, I thought. She really does believe he is a fool. His outfit looked quite ridiculous. All that shocking green, all those hearts, pantomime almost. And his hair as yellow as butter, sticking up as though he had been hit by lightning. He looked as though he had stepped from the pages of a fairy tale, but I wasn't sure what character he was.

The crowd tittered playfully, an obedient audience to Lady Clarence. I could see Doctor Cherrytree behind her, watching carefully. And he wasn't laughing. Lady Clarence handed her champagne glass to Elijah to hold, another act of humiliation. This evening was really all about her. She was quite a lot taller than Loveheart, her gown heavy and wide. She was filling space and she was the only female in the room. Queen bee and her boys. And there was Mr Loveheart, the defective worker bee, floating, alien like. Hovering like an assassin.

"Your father, Lord Loveheart," she continued, as smug as a bug, "was a sensible, reliable and wise man." Her eyes lowered playfully, every compliment a reversed insult to Loveheart. "He was a patron of the arts and was always elegantly dressed." Gentle laughter crept out of the audience. And yet Mr Loveheart remained quite still. "He will always have a place in our hearts."

The audience applauded her.

Mr Loveheart bowed very low. "I am afraid, madam, that none of us have our hearts anymore."

"What a curious remark," she replied.

"Do you think it's going to kick off?" said Walnut quietly from beside me. I really had no idea. I couldn't predict anything Mr Loveheart would do. He could walk away laughing. He could have killed everyone in the room. I almost felt concern for him and I'm not sure why. My own world felt suddenly very small and very ordinary. I am a detective. I look for clues, I arrest criminals, I uphold the law of England. This was outside of my world and my own understanding. I was essentially useless in this situation. My own power limited. I was only an observer; he wanted me to observe.

A hand patted me on the shoulder. It was Doctor Cherrytree. "Detective, I wonder if I could have a private word with you upstairs."

I told Constable Walnut to wait downstairs for me, and I followed the doctor up the stairs, past more of Elijah's portraits of lords and ladies, some with little dogs, others with hunting rifles posed like kings and queens. Captured in time. Captured within the canvas. On to the balcony we stood under the gigantic portrait of Lady Clarence, heavy and imposing. I could almost feel her weight upon me, suffocating. It was as though she was floating, like a deity, and we were within a chapel, her acolytes below, rubbing their hands, dizzy with religious fervor.

Doctor Cherrytree tapped the rail of the balcony with his long, pale fingers. "I'm not sure how you managed to get into this private exhibition but–"

I interrupted him, "I was sent an invitation."

"By whom?"

"It was anonymous."

"I find that extremely hard to believe. In any case, it's most inappropriate for you to be here. You have accused and insulted our members with the most ludicrous theories. I can't have Lady Clarence upset."

"You really all believe you can outwit Death?"

Doctor Cherrytree looked a little taken aback by this remark, and then smirked, "I want you to leave, detective. And take that stupid constable with you."

"I'm not leaving and my constable is certainly not stupid. He has an appreciation of the arts. Although I am beginning to wonder if this really is an art exhibition."

Then he pushed me. I was surprised at how strong he was and I felt myself falling over the balcony. I grabbed at the rail but he shoved me over. I caught sight of his expression: he was manic, his teeth gritted. I grabbed hold of his neck and pulled him with me.

It was a long drop. As I was falling I could see the painting of Lady Clarence, the smug goddess waiting to hear my neck break. I could see Mr Loveheart in the crowd, he was behind Elijah.

We fell to the floor with a thud. We had landed on top of Elijah with a horrible crunching sound. There was a scream from Lady Clarence. I was in pain. Constable Walnut was helping me up. Doctor Cherrytree was crawling off towards the other side of the room. Elijah lay still, his neck twisted, his eyes blank. He looked like a squashed blackbird.

"Constable Walnut," I shouted. "Arrest Doctor Cherrytree for attempted murder!"

"Yes, sir," said Walnut, and leapt on the doctor who was hobbling off into the side room. Walnut had hold off him and dragged him to his feet. "Come here you slippery bugger!"

I could see Mr Loveheart helping himself to the trifle, an especially large portion, and looking very pleased with himself.

Inspector Salt

It was ten o'clock at night by the time we had stuffed the dubious Doctor Cherrytree in a cell. I had been nursing my sore arm, and Constable Walnut brought me in a cup of tea and a sticky bun. All was well with the world. Constable Walnut sat down to join me.

"That was quite an evening, sir."

"What did you think of the exhibition?" I said, sinking my teeth into the bun.

"I'm more of an Expressionist, sir. Distorted for emotional effect."

There was a knock at the door and Inspector Salt entered. Constable Walnut and I rose from our chairs.

"Inspector," I said. He was a tall, thin man with snow-white hair and watery eyes.

"I need a word with you, sergeant. Constable, you can stay put. You need to release Doctor Cherrytree immediately."

"He tried to kill me!" I said, outraged.

"I have spoken to him, and he says it was an accident and you fell, and there are twenty witnesses who say the same thing."

"It wasn't an accident, sir," said Constable Walnut.

"Did you actually witness Doctor Cherrytree push Sergeant White?"

"No, sir, but–"

"Well then. It was an accident. A tragic one."

"Inspector Salt, I have been a detective for Scotland Yard for twenty years and I am not a liar."

"The witnesses say otherwise. You lost your footing and fell. Take a few days off." And at that he produced a pocket watch and clicked it open. It shimmered with weird light. I felt giddy. I felt sick.

"You're… one of them," I said. Constable Walnut looked worried. He had seen the watch and worked it out.

Inspector Salt clicked the time mechanism shut and eyed me coolly. "Like I said. Take a few days off. And we'll say no more about this." He was as cool as an iceberg. My world was collapsing. He left, the door shutting behind him.

I looked to Constable Walnut, "What can we do?"
Walnut replied, selecting another sticky bun. "We could always ask your Mr Loveheart."

VII

Detective Sergeant White Visits Mr Loveheart

I returned to the home of Mr Loveheart. I really had no other place to go. My arm was bandaged in a sling, much like my career – wounded. He stood in the garden in front of the house, waiting for me, waving, wearing a bright yellow waistcoat with buttercups in his hair and a lopsided grin. I wondered if I should slip off home, unnoticed.

"Good morning, detective. How's your arm?"

"Sore." I edged closer to him cautiously.

"Will you be attending the funeral of the man you squashed?"

"No," I sighed. "I have a feeling you pushed Elijah to break my fall."

"Of course. Only happy to help."

"Then help me again. I don't know what to do now."

"Mmmmm," hummed Loveheart, and put his finger to his chin, playing with me. "What do you want to happen?"

"I want all those monsters stopped. I want Lady Clarence and her group punished. But the law can't do it. The law is powerless. I can't do my job. Even my inspector is involved with them."

"Do you want me to get rid of them for you, detective? Are you asking me to murder them for you?"

"I don't know what I'm asking. I need advice. I need some options."

"Your options are limited to say the least. Nasty bunch, that lot. Very unsavoury," he said, glittering like tinfoil.

"Please, whatever you can do."

"I would love to assist you, Detective Sergeant White. I tell you what. I'll decapitate Lady Clarence, Obadiah Deadlock, Edmund Cherrytree and Inspector Salt, who are the main culprits. Their group will fall apart without them. We can't have a member of the police force involved with them – what would Queen Victoria say? In return, you must do me a little favour."

"Which is?"

"In the near future I will need your help, and I

will call upon you. It is a matter very close to my heart." He looked at me almost as though he would burst into tears, and then within an instant he was grinning again.

"All right." We shook hands. A deal had been struck. And I wouldn't regret it.

"Don't ever feel guilt, detective. Remember they are already dead. You are administering natural law and I am your willing assassin."

I felt the greatest sense of relief. He was as mad as a spoon. But he was also oddly heroic and had absolutely no fear of anything. I wondered what on Earth had happened to him to make him into this creature. And I suddenly realised, I think, that I actually liked him.

What on Earth does one wear for a funeral? Something dramatic, obviously. The theme is death. So, black seems obvious, if not a little predictable, and I am not at all predictable. I was of course invited. I am one of the richest men in England and considered an amusing eccentric. So, I can really wear whatever I like. And I can kill whomever I like.

I'd chosen to wear white with, of course, my trademark red hearts. A dashing bachelor!

I'd been mulling over how to kill them all.

DECAPITATION

I simply love the word. Head over heels

I take my ancestral sword with me. Daddy will be so proud that it was going to get some use. Heads lying around the cemetery like pumpkins! I can't wait. I do hope they have an interesting vicar. Maybe one with a lisp. It is going to be a splendid day!

Clippety-clop. Off we trot in my white carriage with white horses. I do like to make an impact. White is so saint-like. So ghostly charming. *Clippety-clop.* To Underwood Church and cemetery. I really could not be late. Important people to kill. Promises to be kept. Keep your fingers crossed, Detective Sergeant White. This one is for you, sir.

It is a beautiful, shiny day in London. My favourite city. My little world. I like to watch the people, the tiny dolls. Puppet people on invisible strings. The bearded ladies dancing in the mud, the rude, misshapen street children, the frog-croaking drunks. All this wickedness of history, layer upon layer of it, like one of Aunt Rosebud's trifles. Poison neatly laid to rest in the layer of custard.

And we arrive at the gates of Underwood Cemetery. A little white church for the elite. Even a rose garden especially for the dead. How very pretty – and they were all hovering about like flies over dung. I could see Lady Clarence in a black gown with a string of pearls, she was weeping on the shoulder of Doctor Cherrytree. What a marvellous actress she would have made. A very sturdy Lady Macbeth, no doubt. Ooooh, and I could see Obadiah Deadlock, that orange-haired fellow on his own. Not much good with company, that one. Maybe he's a bit shy? Even Inspector Salt was there, always good to have a corrupt member of the police force at a mock funeral. And out of the carriage I popped, sword in hand. Am I eccentric enough for you all? I approached them and bowed very low to Lady Clarence. "I really am terribly sorry about the death of Elijah. Have I missed the service?"

Lady Clarence looked at me as though I was a bug to be squashed. She reminded me of Aunt Rosebud in many ways. "Yes. It was a beautiful service," she said, not really looking at me but at an imaginary audience. "We are about to bury him, if you'd like to follow us. If my nerves can stand it – I feel so frail. My poor Elijah. Taken so young."

"Surely not that young, madam," I piped in. "He was a good ripe age." Yes, I imagine he was nearly one hundred.

And all eyes fell upon me. "But his talent will live on. It is certainly burned into my memory!" and I tapped my skull rather animatedly.

At this her lips pursed and she started to move into the cemetery, the rest of her acolytes trailing behind. I could hear Doctor Cherrytree, who was holding her arm, whispering, "Odd fellow, that Loveheart."

Obadiah Deadlock crept up on me. "I do like your sword, Mr Loveheart."

"Oh, thank you very much. I am quite fond of it, myself. Tell me, what's the vicar like?"

"Oh, he's fine. Has a bit of a lisp though."

"Marvellous." I said.

Obadiah scratched his large head, nervously. "I am worried about Lady Clarence. During the service she broke down in tears several times. And she's such a strong lady. Quite formidable, if I dare say."

"Yes, I was just thinking that she reminded me of my Aunt Rosebud."

"Really, was she a formidable woman?"

"Well, she murdered her own children and my mother. But she was extremely good at baking cakes."

"Good grief," cried Obadiah.

"Oh, don't upset yourself, dear fellow. My strange family hasn't affected me in the slightest," and I waved my sword about theatrically.

He didn't respond, oddly enough.

"So," I said, "I hear you're a bit of a star gazer."

"Yes," he replied nervously. "You may have read one of my published works on the theory of time travel."

"Indeed, my father had a keen interest as well. As do I. But I do wonder if humans should be meddling with time at all. Dangerous business, dabbling with the work of the gods."

"Why shouldn't we? It is scientific progress. Evolution."

"At what cost?"

"What do you mean?"

"I mean there is always a price to pay, Mr Deadlock. Always. Tell me, have you ever met Death?"

"Met him? Of course not. He's not a person."

"Oh yes he is, and I've met him. And he's really someone you don't want to annoy."

"I can't continue this conversation, Mr Loveheart. You are talking nonsense. You are talking in riddles." And he moved away from me.

The coffin was white and Lady Clarence laid a single red rose on it, weeping into her enormous bosom. The vicar, a tall, gangly-looking fellow with beady yellow eyes stood at the foot of the grave. I was looking forward to this.

"Iths a thad dhay. The death of Elilah Whhithlle hath moved uth all. Deeply." The vicar's tongue wobbled about his mouth.

Lady Clarence began to wail.

"I know how she feels," I said.

"Elithhahh whath a phhainther. A phhalennted indivduhal..."

I could bear it no more and lopped the vicar's head off with my sword,. It spun into a nearby gravestone, bounced, and then plopped into a hedge.

I then turned to Obadiah and swooshed the sword across his neck, his head dropping neatly into the open grave.

Doctor Cherrytree began to make a run for it – he really was a terrible coward – while Inspector Salt stood in my way. "I am arresting you for murder. Put the sword down, Mr Loveheart. You're obviously having a little turn."

"No, inspector, I am not having a little turn. I am, in fact, on a killing spree." And I chopped his head off too, the blood splattering across myself and Lady Clarence's face. At least she wasn't running away – she was made of stronger stuff. She glared at me instead.

"You stupid little man," she spat. "You're not

going to kill a woman."

"Actually, I've killed several women. And all of them nasty pieces of work, just like you, madam."

"You're a devil!" she cried.

"No, I'm not a devil. Merely a man who is fighting for his soul." I chopped her head off and she sank to her knees. I was covered in blood. I couldn't distinguish the hearts from the blood. I turned to look for Doctor Cherrytree.

But then I heard Bad Daddy speaking.

"Loveheart." It was a voice from the deep dark. It was Mr Fingers. He was leaning against a headstone, smiling gently. "My dear boy. Am I interrupting something?"

"No, does it look like I'm busy?"

"Thought I'd pay you a visit. I need to send you on a little errand."

"Can't you get your other son to do it?"

"You were always my favourite."

"And if I refuse?"

"I will gobble you up." His voice was a black hole in space. And the dead stayed quiet in their graves. "Good boy. Now I have your attention, I need you to go to Whitby. I have found the girl. The girl in the grandfather clock. I need you to bring her here to me."

July 1888
THE CURIOUS CASE OF DAPHNE WITHERS

I was the mistake. I was the ending of the clockmaker. The tickety-tock maker. Little did I know as I was growing up that I would end up in a ladies' watch, with a topaz butterfly gilt in a display cabinet.

Bit of an odd ending, really.

I was twelve years old, small for my age and plain-featured. I had a gift for playing the piano, so I was told, and no brothers or sisters. On my father's birthday I had decided to buy him a pocket watch. A very special one. Recently my parents had hosted a dinner party and one of my father's friends, a Doctor Cherrytree, attended. He had the most beautiful pocket watch. It was silver and engraved with a serpent with ruby eyes. He told me about the clock making shop where he acquired it – and so I decided to find a wonderful gift for my father.

I was wearing a plain white dress, white gloves, and a yellow ribbon in my hair. My hair was very long and the colour of sand. It was the same colour as my grandmother's. The yellow ribbon was a gift from her. It was made of silk and was so soft to touch.

The day was fine, so I walked through the park, the avenue of trees cool and regimented, planted in straight lines.

I had sat and painted watercolours here; but they were not very accomplished, so my tutor informed me. The park was a flat, green, open space with borders of yellow and pink flowers – and paths as unbending as arrows. There were ladies in carriages, wearing pink gloves and fixed smiles. A gentleman on a bicycle rode past me and tipped his hat. He had a dark moustache, hairy and strange, and his teeth were yellow and bent, and I could see the pink tip of his tongue sticking through. It felt like some sort of warning. Some sort of sign.

But I continued down the straight path. It was at times like those I wished I had a brother or sister to take with me, to talk to. I suppose I was quite lonely. I knew I was lucky to live in a nice house with a good family. I was told this regularly by my parents.

I wonder, if you are continuously told how lucky you are, something bad eventually happens.

I was lucky

I was lucky

I was lucky

I

    was

        so

            lucky.

The gentleman on the bicycle rode past me again. This time he was smiling. He circled me with his bike, playfully. Marking out a circle. Enclosing me. I ignored him; I kept my eyes straight ahead on the path through the park. And then he rode off. The danger was gone.

I was lucky.

The path approached the vast flat lake in the centre of the park. I could see a white boat with couples oar-in-hand sail past. The air was calm, the water flickered gently, a few ducks floated past, comfy and quacking. The colours of this park were watery blue and soft greens with a few drops of Turkish delight pink and buttercup yellow, and a great deal of grey. It was a boring watercolour. A bad painting. A line of heavy-laden trees stretched over my head, momentarily putting me into shadow.

Cool and dark. For a moment I felt that heavy shadow over my head, as though the features of my face had disappeared. As though I had gone. As though I was already slipping away out of this life, out of this world. And yet I kept walking.

The darkness made me think about Doctor Cherrytree. He had a face like a shadow, it hides his real intentions. He had clever little dark eyes and a very ugly mouth. Over dinner he was telling my father about his photographs. He takes pictures of souls leaving human bodies. He showed me one of them. It was a picture of an old lady in her armchair. She looked as though she were asleep, a book resting in her lap and over her head a wispy trail of light, which Doctor Cherrytree said was her soul.

I asked him, "Have you trapped her soul in the photograph?" And I remember, that was the point when he took out his pocket watch and checked the time. It was humming like a soft insect. I thought it was the most beautiful thing I had ever seen and he was very pleased that I liked it. He seemed amused by it. The way he looked at me: he saw a plain, not very interesting girl; he saw something empty in me. And I think that's why he let me look at his watch. He let me touch the ruby snake eyes. They were warm, like fire beads. And he took a small card out of his pocket with an address on it and said, "Why don't you get one for your father for his birthday? Here is the address of the shop."

That card was in my purse. It had his fingertip prints on it. Maybe he left a trace of his own soul upon it. And, I wondered, when I die will Mr Cherrytree take a photograph of me?

I walked round the edges of the lake, the path still straight as a line, all clear. I could see the exit; I could see the gates in the distance. Children played on the lawn with a fox-eyed Nanny; a policeman strolled past, eyes ahead, always looking ahead. My feet kept moving, one step after another, as though I were an automaton. I had a wind up clock monkey that walks up and down on the carpet that Daddy got from India. That's what I felt like, now. I was moving but someone else had control over me. I was turning into dark spaces. Emptying.

The rest of my journey I forgot, as though it wasn't important. As though I had been switched off. When I arrived at the clock-maker's shop I felt like I had woken up, and I looked into the window at the beautiful display. They were like precious jewels glinting, touched with something magical. A dark elixir. I found it hard to take my eyes off them. Right in the centre of the display was a silver toad with its mouth open, and inside a clock ticked gently. It made me feel calm, its soft ticking a creepy crawly sleepiness. I opened the door to the shop, the bell above my head ringing, and I knew suddenly.

I was already a dead thing

Albert Chimes was standing in front of me with a strange magnifying eye contraption on his eyes. He was a very old man. His body didn't seem comfortable within its skin, as though it were a bad fit. I think he might have been near to a hundred years old. He looked like a wizard in a fairy tale. One that lives in a strange tower in a forest. A dangerous wizard, who had gone mad, maybe? Is London a great forest? Am I in a magical tower? I think I may have walked into a fairy story.

He took the eye contraption off and smiled politely. "Good morning, young lady. How may I help you?"

I could hear a cat purring, and a slinky plump black-as-night feline materialized on the shelf, watching me with dazzling emerald eyes.

"Her name is Cleopatra. Do you like cats?" His smile remained fixed.

"I have come for a gift for my father. It's his birthday. And yes, I do like cats. She is very pretty."

"What sort of clock would your father like?"

"A pocket watch."

"I have quite a few pocket watches at the moment. Step over here and we'll have a look in the display cabinet."

I crossed to him, where a glass cabinet with a purple velvet lining sat. Inside, a dozen pocket watches were nesting. As comfy as eggs. All of them were made of silver, some with gold threads and jewels. Some had animals carved into them, or symbols: I saw a fox with a diamond tail, a tortoise with a green jewelled shell, one with an eye symbol, another with a row of dancing imps. But in the corner, I saw a watch for my father: it had an engraving of a kingfisher with a key in its mouth. My father had always loved kingfishers.

"That is the one I want," and I pointed to it. Albert Chimes was just about to open the case, when he looked at me rather oddly. The way the man on the bike had looked at me.

Circling me.

PART THREE

I

Mirror & Her Sisters

What is my earliest memory? I remember when I was called Myrtle. That was my name. One of three sisters.

Myrtle Violet Rose.

We were listening to Grandpa tell us a fairy story. It was about a wolf who lived in the forest and he was very hungry. I remember Violet was frightened; she didn't like his big teeth and his big yellow eyes.

Wolves are supposed to love the moon, they are deeply in love with her. She protects them, she gives them power, feeds them with love. Stars tremble about her.

Grandpa says the wolf can disguise himself. He wears the clothes of humans so they can be tricked and eaten. In this story there is a little girl with a red cloak. She carries a hunting knife in case a wolf tries to eat her. A huntsman watches over her, he has a big axe and he knows the forest and can recognize wolves.

Is London a great forest? Are there wolves dressed in top hats? Smiling, eating cake and drinking tea?

My name was Myrtle. I didn't own anything red. The only red was my hair. My sisters' hair was brown. My sisters said fairy folk have red hair. Red as a sacrifice. Am I a piece of meat? Will a handsome wolf man want me for dinner?

Grandpa says the wolf dresses up as the little girl's grandma and sits in bed waiting for her. Granny's shawl on his shoulders, her spectacles perched on the end of his wolfish snout. Tucked up in bed. The moon heavy, prehistoric above him. A night light.

"I don't want her to get eaten," said Rose, and covered her ears.

"If you don't listen to the story, you won't learn anything," Grandpa replied, his yellowish teeth snapping together. What did he want us to learn? Did he want us to carry an axe? What was the lesson?

The moon is always on the side of wolves. The huntsman guards the forest path. If you have tea with a wolfman in a top hat then you will probably be eaten. Maybe the granny wasn't tricked. Maybe she let him in. Maybe there is something inside us that wants to be gobbled up. My sisters were scared of the story, they didn't like wolves. I touched my hair, I could feel the heat, the teasing itch.

And that was my first memory.

My name was Myrtle. When I died, I jumped into a mirror. Became a reflection. Part of the moon. The wolves sing to me at night now.

II

Pomegranate
THE WIFE OF MR FINGERS

I was abducted from a field of flowers when I was sixteen years old. There were poppies in the field, as red as fire. Bursting like blood vessels. I remember that he smelt of angels. My Auntie Eva told me that angels smell like fireworks because the atmosphere burns their wings, crackles them like paper under a lighted match. Auntie Eva said never trust angels because they are beautiful. But he wasn't beautiful. He was small and poisonous with dark spectacles. I wanted him so much to be beautiful.

On hot summer afternoons I used to visit her. She lived in a rundown cottage near the river, cracks in the walls, white paint flaking like old skin. I would touch those walls with my finger, imagining I was touching a tree and trying and guess its age. Ring on ring. She called herself a happy spinster. She hated men and mirrors. She said both were liars.

Sometimes she would make a pot of tea and we would sit and feed the birds in her little garden, mostly blackbirds and one very overweight robin who was her favourite. We sat in a lazy dream listening to the slow fat beat of wings and the soft slithering of snails. Sometimes she would read my palm. She had an interest in the occult. Her grandmother Molly had been a fortune-teller in Brighton on the pier. There was a strange old photograph of her in the hallway with a red turban on her head and a dead stuffed snake coiled in her lap. She looked like a fraud. Auntie Eva would polish her picture every spring like an ornament to make sure Grandma Molly could keep a watchful eye over us. I wondered why. There really was nothing much to see.

The cottage was small and painted with the colour of sunflowers, which had faded over the years into a smoker's-finger yellow. The furniture was all from philanthropic charities, a broken sofa with a floral print and a ringworm occasional table. Wonky legged chairs and a strange squashy cushion seat with bumblebees embroidered on it, flying in circles. Her strange assortment of relatives adorned the walls in old frames, a photograph of Grandma

Molly's father, Reginald Crump, a taxidermist who was hung for poisoning his wife. Reggie's portrait was appropriately hung in the outdoor privy. In Aunt Eva's bedroom, in a beautiful ornate frame decorated with dragonflies coiling like the fingers of a magician, danced around a picture of twin baby boys in a pram. The names underneath read *Arthur & Goliath, Cairo 1850*. Their father was as rich as a prince and was an explorer and archaeologist and his name was Gawain Honey-Flower, a huge man who had travelled out to Cairo and, as Aunt Eva fondly recalled, met a beautiful Egyptian woman, plump as a pagan goddess. The story changed depending on how much wine Aunt Eva had drunk. Sometimes she was "a witch, who had caught Gawain's soul in a mirror", other times "the daughter of a pig farmer, who had a toothy grin like a carved pumpkin on Halloween". Either way, the fate of their children remained the same on each story telling. A year later the twins were born: Arthur who sucked his fingers and Goliath who gobbled everything up just like a bear cub.

Goliath was sent to a boys' school in England whilst Arthur trained with his father as an archaeologist and participated in the excavations of the tombs of the Pharaohs and the deciphering of hieroglyphics. At the age of 22, whilst exploring the Nile with a French aristocrat, he fell in whilst drunk and was eaten by a crocodile. Goliath was Aunt Eva's favourite relative because he was "physically enormous and hairy", two attributes which she thought of as wondrous. The remaining less interesting relatives were spotted throughout the house: a sturdy housekeeper, a balding pharmacist, a non-descript postman, a shrivelled florist and finally, lurking rather suspiciously in a mother of pearl frame by the cat flap, an incredibly ugly coffin maker. I wondered where she would end up putting me.

Aunt Eva was a great collector of knick-knacks and loved roaming round the flea markets, sometimes picking up the most disgusting and unusual items. In her kitchen drawer was a jar with floating glass eyeballs, a pair of birthing stirrups and a quack doctor's prescription: Dr Tumbleweeds "Magical Remedy" for ailments of the heart, as thick and black as syrup. I opened it once, it stank of toffee apples and something rotting. On her bedroom table sat an assortment of coloured glass perfume bottles, aquamarine, ruby red, snail silver, flamenco pink. Little magic jars, each with a strange smell: peaches and cream, mothballs, lavender and butterfly wings, tickling the nostrils. On her hand mirror there was a picture of her and my mother when they were my age, wearing strange dresses and holding hands. I examined the photograph carefully; they were almost identical, it was only the sly look in Aunt Eva's eye that gave her identity away. My mother never looked sly, always calm, always snow white.

The river curled round the bottom of Auntie's garden, lapping like a greedy tongue. It was deep and thick water, full of glittering slime and snake-tail weeds. Her garden was on a slope, descending into the riverbank where great spongy heaps of frogspawn floated, soft and glistening. Occasionally we would see a little boat sail along the river, with a red sail. The man in it was a local, Mr Wishbone. He caught freshwater fish and slept on his boat. I waved to him once but he ignored me. I thought he looked hundreds of years old, like a moth-eaten wizard. Perhaps if you gazed into his eyes, you would turn into nothing. Aunt Eva had told me he's an old miserable bastard and if he ever moored his boat at the bottom of her garden she would drill a hole in it and watch him sink.

On one afternoon that she read my palm, she opened a bottle of red wine and, after a few generous glasses, held my hand like a prayer book, studying the lines, the hidden words, the invisible threads of me. And she always said the same thing – "Someone is coming for you; he has ladybirds in his eyes." – and then she laughed sadly.

"Is it a handsome prince?" I would say. She looked away from me. I took my hand away like a book that has been read and discarded. The little rituals we went through, they were always the same. As if we were both waiting for something to happen, something that, like lightning, would strike and leave a terrible imprint upon us. While we waited, we played these games.

The village in which we live was called Appledoor and was a small, sleepy-eyed place surrounded by fields of apple trees and ancient woodland. I had always felt as safe as a bed bug in this place. Snuggled up, squashed with love. But on the day of my sixteenth birthday things began to change. There was a great thunderstorm that day: black ribbons of darkness spread across the sky and the clouds were shaped like dragons, soaring and screaming. That evening the schoolmaster, Mr Quipple, was found drowned in the river. He had committed suicide, left no note.

Aunt Eva thought he was suspicious because he never grew any flowers in his garden. She said on

Sundays he would read his newspaper in the garden and shout at the local tomcat if it was lazing about. She says that men who have gardens without any flowers or plants have no soul. She said the tomcat probably pushed him in the river. Or a mermaid lured him in, swishing her aquamarine tail and fluttering her moon-silver eyelashes at him. She kept the newspaper article of his death in the toilet next to our ancestor, Reginald Crump.

I asked her if anything else awful ever happened in this town and she said no, but she suspected the meat at the local butchers. "It's probably human," she said, then laughed out loud, a shocking laughter with hints of electricity in it that zapped and tingled.

She has a huge mane of thick hair that she dyes a vibrant flame red and crimps. It falls down to her waist like crazy snakes. I think she really is a beautiful woman. She's something strange from a fairy tale, or maybe she's Queen Titania. She's made of raw magic and rare delights. She has just turned fifty and says she has never been in love. I don't know if this makes her sad. I don't really know how to feel about it at all. I think magical creatures find it difficult to live amongst humans, in a human world. She must be so frustrated. She must be so lonely. But she won't tell me.

My mother is not beautiful like her sister, Eva. She is a tall, strong woman and a wonderful gardener. Hands always in the earth. Hands always making something grow. She campaigns for the suffragettes. I have no father. My mother told me he was a salesman just passing through Appledoor. He wooed her with magic tricks and then got her pregnant and left. There are no pictures of him, only her memories.

She said he was handsome with a lopsided smile and full of promises. And full of shit, as Aunt Eva often tells me. I am like my mother, tall and plain. My eyes are very pale, like a ghost. My mother tells me I have my father's eyes. Hers are baby blue. They are the colour of safety and calm waters. Mine are the colour of moth wings, hiding and fluttering in a secret wardrobe. Just like Daddy.

On the day of my abduction, the sun was boiling like an egg. The hottest day on record for fifty years. I woke up sweating, my thighs damp. I'd dreamt that Aunt Eva was a mermaid swimming in the river, throwing insults at Mr Wishbone in his boat. I dreamt that mother was standing in a field of bright golden corn and that Daddy came to visit me, came into my room with a basket of apples. He said he knew a magic trick and he waved his hand over those green apples and they turned into bright red pomegranates, heavy magic orbs. He said they were delicious, "Why don't you taste one, sweetheart?" His hair was greasy and his hands nervous. I thought, he's just a con man. He's a grin without a face. Something not to be trusted.

I heard Aunt Eva's voice, like a soft siren coming from the waters, "Oh, my poor girl. That bastard. That bastard. He's sold you." The dream ended. I heard my mother leave the house and the neighbours' dog howl. I pulled myself out of bed and stood in front of my mirror, examining myself. I thought, I have not been ravished yet, I wonder what it would feel like. I was sixteen and I had not been kissed. In fact, no boys had ever shown any interest in me at all.

I am only sixteen;
> *there is plenty of*
>> *time.*

I sat with Aunt Eva in her garden. She made homemade lemonade and put something alcoholic in it. She wore an extravagant, very low cut green dress with a string of fake pearls. She smelt of honey and spices. The heat beat down on us; we were two eggs in a frying pan sizzling gently. A quill rested in her hand like a wand, tapping against the garden chair. I think she would be capable of serious witchcraft. She wiped her lips with her sleeve and looked at me. "Darling child. Do you know that I own a shotgun?" I shook my head, I didn't. She looked at me quite seriously. I could feel some dark magic humming under her words.

"I want you to listen very carefully to me, Pomegranate. I think something very bad is going to happen to you today. I have heard it in dreams. I have seen it in the smile of cats. Read it in the frog spawn." She sat back into her sun chair and glugged down the remainder of her lemonade. I didn't know whether to be worried or to laugh.

"Will you protect me, Auntie, with your shotgun?" I said, almost mocking her.

She stared at me. She had something alien in her eyes, something from a remote star.

"When he comes for you, I will be with you, and I will stop it."

A long silence ensued between us. I could hear the wind pick up over the water, rustling, secretive. A cool sleepiness. She yawned and brushed strands of hair out of her eyes and then smiled a deep secret smile like a crocodile, and looked upon me. "I am going to tell you a story about me and your mother, when we were young girls in Appledoor. Would you like that, Pomegranate?"

"Yes," I said, not really thinking. The sun was in my eyes, making me sleepy, making me dizzy. And so she began. She told me the tale, which she had told me many times. She told me the tale of the Lightning Tree in the field of flowers. And she said when she had finished the tale, she would take me to the field and show me the tree. And so I listened. I shut my eyes and let myself slip into the words, like maple syrup oozing over pancakes, with satisfying easiness.

When Eva and my mother were ten years old they went to live in a foundlings home called Honeybee House, the other side of the river. Their parents, my grandparents, had died in an accident. A train had derailed off a bridge; they had been trapped inside and drowned. Eva and mother never talk about their parents and they have no pictures of them. I wonder sometimes if they ever existed, if they are both strange women from another galaxy, touched with stardust. Maybe all my ancestors are borrowed from other people, photographs Aunt Eva has collected from her flea markets and adopted – made into an intricate jigsaw past. A fake scrapbook of memories. I wonder then, who are these women really? Maybe they are not human. Maybe they are the daughters of gods dropped from the heavens. And then, what would that make me?

The Lightning Tree

Aunt Eva – as lazy as a cat, as beautiful as fire roses, as mad as the buzzing of bees – began her story. A mile outside Appledoor was a huge field, lush with wild grasses, with a solitary tree. A tree that had been hit by lightning and was black as charcoal and fifty feet high. If you placed your hands on it, it felt warm. Like apple pie from the oven. And it smelt. It smelt of syrup and of blood. When Aunt Eva and mother were little girls they would come and visit the tree and play in its branches. They would cast spells by its roots and make wishes in its secret holes. It never spoke to them. It just listened and watched. Aunt Eva said she would leave secret messages for her sister, and sometimes gifts. Once she hung a jade hairpin from its branches, a dangling gift on a pink ribbon.

On the summer of their eighteenth birthdays, my father arrived into the village selling soap, and wooed my mother with his crooked charming smile and perfumed words. He stayed clear of Aunt Eva. He was frightened of her, thought she was a witch. He thought of her as one of those women too beautiful for men. Only the gods would touch her. My mother took my father to show him the lightning tree. He had no interest in such things. He held her hand by the roots of that tree, promised her a thousand things and then fucked her. It was over quickly. He left in the morning, soap samples jiggering in his bag.

But Aunt Eva had done something. She had carved an image of him out of the tree. She had dug in the earth where he had cum by the roots and smeared it over the doll. And she had chanted under a red moon and hung him from the tree. While my mother wept, pregnant with me, Eva was enforcing revenge. And the gods listened to her.

He was made impotent and diseased. And Aunt Eva laughed. And the gods laughed. And my mother wept.

A few years later, to return himself to full health my father, a born salesman, struck a deal with a demon. In exchange for sex. And today, Aunt Eva reminded me, was the day of collection.

We walked out of the village, hand in hand. Aunt Eva's hair as red as fire, my own pale, and in comparison, uninteresting. Through the fields, lush with wildflowers, bordered with ancient woodlands. It was sizzling hot, scissor hot. As hot as Eva's hair. The weather for devils to play in. The sky was heart pink, the air smelt of cinnamon cakes, so sweet and hot. It was as though I was falling under a spell.

"Tell me about this man who is coming to collect me, Auntie," I said. And she turned to me and replied, "He is the Lord of the Underworld. He lives in a palace of clocks. He has an obsession with time and with ladybirds."

"How do you know all this?"

"The gods talk to me in dreams. Tell me things I shouldn't know."

"Why does he like ladybirds?"

"I was told by my mother when I was a little girl that ladybirds are little witches. Maybe that's why he likes to collect them."

And we walked into the field where the lightning tree stood amidst an ocean of bursting poppies, little flames burning through the grasses, thousands and thousands of them. We walked through them, as though we were walking through fire, our hands brushing their soft heads, all that red and black, like ladybirds. The colour of the underworld. The tree had a door on it. It was a portal. We sat and waited by the roots in the field of fire flowers. Flowers like bloodstains on a bedsheet.

"Will it hurt?" I said.

"Only the first time," Aunt Eva replied.

The door opened and out he stepped. A small man, dark haired, black spectacles with a waistcoat covered in tiny ladybirds. He was ugly to me and I was much taller than him. I felt repulsion. He reminded me of dead things: rotten fungi, withered nettles and tripe. He was sticking in my throat and he was enjoying seeing me sickened. He approached us, soft footed, admiring the view of poppies.

"Pomegranate. How lovely to meet you at last. You are not beautiful, but that really doesn't matter," and he smiled, sourly.

Aunt Eva spoke. "Will you make a deal with me to save her from this?"

The Lord of the Underworld examined her carefully. "You are a ladybird," and he circled her excitedly. I did not excite him at all. "I am afraid there are no deals to be struck. A deal was made with her father. I cannot break such a contract."

"I will go in her place," Aunt Eva replied.

"So tempting an offer. I would love to have you

in my kingdom. In my bedchamber, ladybird. But I cannot."

Aunt Eva approached him and placed her hand on his heart and he started to scream. She was speaking magic words. The sky broke into lightning flashes, dozens of them, electrical frenzy. I hunched by the roots of the tree, crying, terrified as my Aunt held the Lord Of the Underworld. Her hand gripping his hair in her hands. It was killing her. The gods watched on, and they didn't know who would win.

And then he grabbed her and kissed her deeply, sucking the life from her. And she fell to the ground in the field of poppies, as though a sleeping princess. I thought, what passion he has for her. No one will ever feel like that for me. And she turned into poppies.

"Don't worry, Pomegranate. I have put her under an enchantment, turned her into flowers. She is not dead. I could not kill something that wonderful."

Then he took me by the hand and led me through the doorway into his world.

A Room Full of Pomegranates

The bedchamber of the Lord of the Underworld had ladybirds on everything. Embroidered on the pillowcases, crawling up the curtains, dancing over the mirror.

He takes me to bed. I can hear all those clocks ticking. He hurts me and then he does it again and again. Locks me in the room. He had no other use for me.

I am told I am his wife. I am the wife of the Lord of the Underworld.

The room has little paintings, which hang on the wall – each created in dark oils and each one a picture of a pomegranate. Each one a picture of me, I suppose. There must be a hundred of them. Each one beautiful and sinister. The seeds of the pomegranates are eyes; I am watched from every corner of the bedroom by his spies.

I open a little jewelled box and inside it rest a sharp letter opener, encrusted with ruby jewels.

I stab myself in the heart.

I am floating on the boat of Mr Wishbone, the boat with the little red sail. It is the red of a pomegranate. It is so peaceful, the waters gentle, the air smells of milk, such wonderful softness.

We are sailing away, we are sailing into space.

III

Mr Fingers Attempts to Retrieve His Wife

I awoke in the field of poppies. My Aunt had been turned into flowers and I was alone.

I ran back to Aunt Eva's cottage. I ran as fast as I could and locked myself in. Into her bedroom, under the covers I hid. I wished I could have changed into different shapes. I wish I was magical like Aunt Eva and could fight him, but all I could do was run away. I fell asleep and dreamt I was back in the room surrounded by pictures of pomegranates. Their eyes were full of ladybirds, fat ruby shapes opening their wings. I shouted out for Aunt Eva to save me but she had turned into a goddess in a coffin made of red flowers. And the poppies were laughing, the lightning tree was laughing, the pomegranates were laughing and he was coming back for me, he was coming back to teach me a lesson.

When I woke up, the moon had risen in the sky, a silver sickle, glinting like a scimitar. I descended the staircase and into the kitchen to make a pot of tea. Dried lavender and sage hung in bunches from the window and pots of fresh mint sat by the sink, a stone frog peered at me, propping the door ajar. This was a witch's kitchen. Why did I not inherit any magic? Moonlight drifted lazily through the room and it was then I heard the knocking at the door. I let him in. What else could I do?

He examined me like a sleepy spider and sat himself at the kitchen table, while I poured the tea. One of Aunt Eva's fruit cakes sat like a heavy omen near the teapot.

"I am not accustomed to my wives committing suicide to escape me. That will not happen again, do you understand?"

I did not answer him.

He adjusted his spectacles. "Of course, I don't want you to be unhappy. I know that you will be lonely in the Underworld and so I have decided to grant you six months of every year on Earth, and then you will return to me for the following six. If you disobey me again, I will break this agreement. Will you agree to this?"

I nodded my head.

"You are not overly intelligent and you are not very interesting, but you are my wife, my possession, and we must try to be civil to one another."

"What about my Aunt Eva?" I asked.

"For the six months you spend with me in the Underworld she will remain as poppies, under my enchantment. When you return to the Earth, she will transform back. And I realize she may very well try to kill me again, which I greatly look forward to," and he smiled slyly. He continued, "I am not overly fond of women, but I could become very attached to her. She has a spark about her."

"Perhaps you should seek the company of men. My Aunt has some lovely gowns upstairs you could try on," and I laughed.

He slapped me across the face so hard I fell onto the floor. "Watch your tongue."

I stood up rather shakily. "May I get some clothes from upstairs before we leave?"

He nodded, not even bothering to look at me. I walked steadily up the staircase into Aunt Eva's bedroom and took the shotgun from under her bed. As I walked downstairs I pointed the gun at his head. He looked genuinely surprised. I pulled the trigger and his head exploded all over the wall. "That's for slapping me, you pile of dogshit!"

I kept hold of the shotgun and ran back out of the town into the field of poppies. Aunt Eva was standing up, her hair alive like flames, poppies still scattered over her body plopping gently to the earth. She hugged me, half in a daze.

"I shot him, Aunt Eva. I blew his head off."

She answered, "He won't be dead."

"I don't want to go back with him," I screamed. Poppies were still attached to her hair, which was long, blood red like lava. Suddenly, through a haze of poppy heads, he appeared and seized her by the hair, twisting it in his hands. I held the shotgun up again but I couldn't get a clear shot between the two of them. Aunt Eva shouted something out and lightning started to dance in the skies and it fell, bolt after bolt onto him. Electrified, he flew off her and I shot him again, his head exploding. His headless body fell backwards, softly, into the poppies.

"What do we do now, Aunt Eva?"

"We stuff him in the tree," she cried, grabbing his feet. "It will hold him as a coffin." And so we stuffed his body into the whorl of the tree and filled it with soil, and Aunt Eva bound it with a heavy charm of poppies.

We could hear him screaming in the tree: *"Bitches!"*

We left that field of poppies and went home. Aunt Eva burnt black candles and sage and charmed little bells round the cottage. She painted spiral symbols on my face and arms with ink and I fell asleep on the sofa. And we waited.

Mr Fingers in the Tree

Bitches
　　B
　　　i
　　　　t
　　　　　c
　　　　h
　　　　　e
　　　　　s
　　　　　　　B
　　　　　　　　I
　　　　　　T
　　　　　　　C
　　　　　　　H
　　　　　　　　E
　　　　　　　　　S
　　　　　　　　BITCHES

IV

Queen of the Underworld, What Will Become of Me?

I told Aunt Eva about the sex. I told her everything. She was not surprised. We waited three days. We remained in the cottage. We stayed quiet. He remained imprisoned in the tree. The ink spirals on my face and arms became smudged like a child's drawing. I was a messy picture book. Aunt Eva didn't let my mother see me. She kept her away with pretty lies. She was too convincing. "So your Mother won't worry," she said and she was right, yes, she was right.

"I am frightened. What's going to happen?"

Aunt Eva looked up, as though she was reading the marks on the ceiling, her eyes staring into something. She reminded me of a crocodile, glassy eyed, guarding the entrance to a pyramid marked with hieroglyphs. She had teeth. She replied, 'He's very angry. I don't think that tree will hold him much longer."

I was crying then. He would kill me, I knew it. And she put her arms around me, circled me with her hair which smelt of cinder and she whispered, "Do not be afraid."

"Can you see into the future, can you see what will happen?"

"Only glimpses, Pomegranate. But I will fight for you. You have been unlucky. Your father sold you to a shit." And we both laughed. For there was nothing else left to do but laugh. And she stroked my face with her cool hand.

"Have you ever been in love, Aunt Eva?"

"No," she said. "But I was hurt once and I never let it happen again."

"Tell me about it," I asked. "If only so I can forget for a while."

And she told me the story. She was seventeen and she had a secret. She had met a young aristocrat riding in the woods one day. She said his horse was as white as wedding dresses. She never knew his name. Sometimes she thought he never really existed, as though he were formed from her imagination, summoned on dandelion wishes: spongy fairy wings blown into the wind to stop her loneliness. He used to gallop around her, throw flowers in her hair and blow her kisses. He used to tell her he loved her, over and over. He used to play games with her, toy with her, stir her up. This happened for weeks and weeks.

One day Aunt Eva found him in the woods, playing games with another girl. And he saw Aunt Eva watching him. And he tried to smile. He tried so very hard but the look on her face was something he hadn't seen before. It wasn't anger or jealousy. It wasn't sadness or heartbreak. For Aunt Eva was smiling. She was smiling the most terrible smile. Like a crocodile.

"He was a coward," she said. "He was the most terrible coward."

"What did you do?"

"I took my revenge," she said quietly.

"How?"

Her words were so soft. Her teeth were so sharp. "I burnt his ancestral home to the ground. I killed his parents and his sister. I hunted him down, played games with him, toyed with him, butchered him and ate his heart."

"Do you think that was perhaps an overreaction?" I said, stupefied.

"He cried at the end. He cried so much. The fucking coward." She was deep in her memories.

And then she looked sadly at me. "Pomegranate, listen to me. If a man hurts you – cut him down. If a man humiliates you – cut him down. If a man plays games with you – cut him down."

"What are you going to do with my husband?"

There was a knocking at the door. Aunt Eva turned gently towards me, smiling. "Something worse." She opened the door and my husband entered and sat himself once again at the kitchen table. I stayed where I was on the sofa.

"Let me tell you what is going to happen now, ladies," he said with the utmost control, the teapot on the table exploding into pieces. "I am taking my ugly wife Pomegranate back to the Underworld where I will put her through a variety of experimental degradations. As for you," he glanced at Aunt Eva, "I am going to have you put in a cage where I can watch you starve to death."

"I would very much like to see you try, you little turd."

He stood, screaming "I AM THE LORD OF THE UNDERWORLD AND YOU WILL DO WHAT I SAY OR I WILL TEAR YOU APART!"

The cottage shook, the walls shook, the windows exploded. Aunt Eva looked at me, "Run back to your mother, go now!"

And I ran out of the house. I could see her turn into fire. A burning goddess. A wall of flames. I ran down the path. I could see the cottage on fire, an inferno. The cottage was sinking into the earth, forming a crater as if a meteorite had struck.

I ran back to mother, who was baking bread. I had no idea what to say to her.

Mr Fingers & Aunt Eva

F
  a
    l
    l
     i
      n
       g
        into the Underworld.

Prince Number 9 saw them drop into the black river surrounding the palace. He watched from his turret. He said they were both made of fire, like angels falling. Made a big *splosh!* They both dragged themselves from the waters, soggy and slipping. And he said Daddy looked really pissed off. We all wanted to know who she was, the lady with the red hair. We were told later she was a witch trying to ruin Daddy's marriage. She must have succeeded because we never saw his wife again.

So what happened to the witch, you ask? Well at first Daddy didn't know what to do with her. She was a difficult guest and prisoner. He kept threatening to put her in a cage, but he never did. She in turn had done some real damage to him. She had cut off the entrance to the Upperworld and we were all now trapped.

Prince Number 2 got a clout round the ear for asking Daddy if he would marry the witch. I kept my mouth shut, but I wanted to speak to her. And one day I got my chance.

She was sitting in the garden under an apple tree and she looked rather annoyed. I took the opportunity to introduce myself. "Hello, my name is Prince Number 14, or Loveheart if you prefer," and I smiled as nicely as I could. She had very unusual eyes – they reminded me of something predatory, something reptilian perhaps. She looked at me carefully, brushing tendrils of red hair out of her face.

"Hello, Loveheart," she said.

"So, how are you enjoying the Underworld?"

She looked into me momentarily and pointed a finger upwards. "You are also from up there."

"Yes," I said. "Daddy kidnapped me and murdered my real father."

"Sadly, I am not surprised by that remark. He's not a gentleman, has no idea about good manners."

"Can you open the doorway to the Upperworld?"

She looked suspiciously at me, "Maybe."

"So why don't you do it and go home?"

"I am protecting someone I love. I will not open anything until I know she will be safe."

"Is the Lord of the Underworld in love with you?"

"Not at all. He is obsessed with me because he cannot control me. That is all."

"Oh," I said, not really knowing how to reply.

"He has no understanding of love and he doesn't like women very much," and she laughed to herself.

"Why is that funny?" I asked.

"Well, he kidnaps women to be his wives, without much liking them to start with. And then kidnaps children, calling them numbers, again without really liking them at all. What *does* he actually like, I wonder?"

"He likes clocks," I said.

"No, he likes the fact that clocks are predictable. Controllable. He has no understanding of time, either. He is rather stupid." And her eyes wandered off into the distance.

"What are you thinking about?" I asked.

"I was just imagining him in a dress." And I left her to her imagination under the apple tree and thought her wondrous.

Prince Number 3 spied on her, watched her from the turrets, sent blackbirds out to send back reports. There was a standoff between Daddy and the witch. Neither would back down. The portal remained shut. And then one day something changed.

Daddy made a mistake.

He slapped her across the face
    and I remember
        that she was
           smiling.

She massacred Princes 1 to 12. Picked them off one by one. Chopped their heads off and put them on Daddy's dining table. It was then he started to beg. My life and Tumbletee's were spared. The marriage contract was broken and the portal finally opened.

I want to be just like her when I grow up.

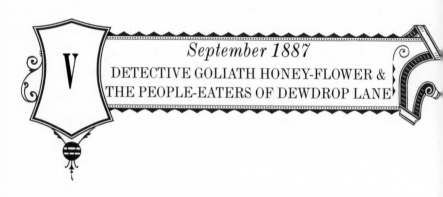

My life before I met Mirror was very different. I was a detective with Scotland Yard for some years in London. A few weeks before I met her, I was assigned to a very peculiar case.

It was autumn in London, great heavy bundles of chocolate and burnt toffee leaves lay across the streets, blown in the wind. The skies, grey and swirling, were streaked with ribbons of violent pink. My detective sergeant, Percival White, had assigned me to a case regarding an elderly couple who lived on Dewdrop Lane, which was a rundown little terraced road in south London, near a boatyard. For weeks the neighbours had been complaining about this elderly couple. Noises in the night, banging and screaming. And strange smells. I had been sent round there to talk to the couple and find out exactly what was going on and to sort it out. It was supposed to be straightforward.

When I arrived at the home of the Crumb siblings, it was raining so heavily that my umbrella broke under the weight of the painfully big wet splodges of rainfall, and lay in my hands like a drowned blackbird. Disposing of the umbrella in a convenient bin, I approached the small terraced house and knocked on the door. My knuckles were bruised, for in the evenings I had been boxing, something my father had trained me to do in Egypt.

I could hear a soft shuffling from within, a pair of slippers moving over a carpet, approaching slowly. That morning I had been reading a letter from my father. The pages were folded like a handkerchief in my pocket, near my heart. He had begun an excavation in Cairo on the tomb of an Egyptian princess. It would take many months to complete, but he was overjoyed. He was hoping I would come back to Cairo and stay with him, something I had promised. My father's handwriting was swirling and beautiful, with hieroglyphics dotted about the corners: magic symbols.

I missed him. I missed Egypt. He had sent me some of his sketches of the finds near the entrance to the tomb and of the wall engravings. Red and black ladybird-like creatures dancing over the entrance, sketched hurriedly. Comical drawings of priests wearing insect-like masks lined the walls in some sort of procession, each carrying a jar containing something belonging to the princess. Each of these priests displayed with a ceremonial dagger and a mirror. My father had told me they carried mirrors to catch souls within, and they also acted as doorways into other worlds and as divination tools. I wondered about the princess and the power she held over these men. How far would they go for her? Was there a limit at all?

The door opened with a slight creak and Dotty Crumb, a tiny woman dressed in a pink dressing gown and oversized fluffy slippers, peered curiously at me.

"Good afternoon, Miss Crumb. My name is Detective Goliath Honey-Flower. I'm here about the complaints."

Her lips curved into a crescent moon, her eyes were very pale, egg-like. "Oh yes, do come in," she chirped. Her voice reminded me of a child; it didn't belong in her body. I followed her into the hallway, where a shabby birdcage hung, now empty. "I've made jam tarts, they are Mortimer's favourite," she said, patting me gently on the shoulder. In the small kitchen sat Mortimer Crumb, long and lean, almost skeletal, wearing a long, brown oversized coat. He had a small bird-like face and very large, long teeth.

I was guided to a seat by Dotty, while a cup of tea was poured for me out of a cracked teapot and a jam tart plopped on a plate in front of my eyes. Mortimer extended his hand towards mine, "A pleasure to meet you, sir."

The kitchen was small and dark with tobacco-stained wallpaper and a framed picture of Her Majesty Queen Victoria, wearing a grimace, hanging lopsidedly over the sink. Glancing outside the window, there was a tiny garden overrun with weeds. Behind Mortimer was another hallway leading to a staircase, and beneath that a green door, which I assumed must lead to the basement. What caught my eye was the ornate gold lock on this door.

Mortimer wiped jam from his lips and spoke. "May I ask where you originate from, Mr Honey-Flower?"

I took a sip of the tea, which was very well stewed. "I was born in Egypt, but my father was English." The chair underneath me creaked with my weight. I caught my reflection in the mirror; my beard was damp and dishevelled. I looked like a great bear that had fallen into the river. The siblings stared at me mischievously.

"For the last few weeks we have been receiving complaints from your neighbours about noises at night coming from your house. Screaming and banging, mostly. Can you explain any of this?"

Mortimer scratched his nose. "We have a problem with this house. We believe that there is a malignant presence here."

"Malignant presence?" I replied.

"Yes, we've been hearing strange noises, and we have heard our names called out on several occasions."

"And don't forget the smell, dearie," said Dotty. "A terrible whiff, like burning pig flesh."

"Are you suggesting your home is haunted?"

"That's correct, Mr Honey-Flower," said Mortimer, helping himself to another jam tart. "We have had a very quiet life, my sister and I. We have lived in this house since we were children and there have never been any problems. The first occurrence happened at Christmas, when Dotty was preparing dinner in the kitchen and she heard something call her name. I also heard a voice. I was reading the paper. We had a cat and a song thrush in a little cage, and both disappeared soon after."

"Anything else?"

"My sister and I don't dream any more."

There was a queer silence. Mortimer was munching on his jam tart. Dotty tapped her bony finger against her cheek. Mortimer suddenly laughed and Dotty giggled like a schoolgirl. I found them both somewhat unnerving.

Mortimer adjusted his coat, which was spotted with jam, and leaned forward towards me.

"So, are we being haunted, Detective Honey-Flower? Have we offended a dead relative?"

"Yes, perhaps Great Aunt Margery," Dotty said slyly. "She never liked us as children, do you remember the incident with the tea cosy?"

The chair beneath me creaked painfully. I could feel one of the legs wobble nervously. "I am not an expert on the paranormal."

"What are we dealing with, detective?" Mortimer said, gazing into me. His eyes were small glimmering things, like faerie gold.

"What is behind the green door?" I said, without realising the words had left my mouth. I could feel the letter in my jacket; it was like a hot water bottle over my heart. I could smell a rich sweetness in the air, a thick heavy scent that was overpowering and covering up the stink of something else.

"That will be the tapioca pudding ready then." Dotty gleefully spooned a huge mass of frog spawn creamy steaming pudding into three bowls and handed one to me.

"Oh really, I couldn't manage any more."

"Don't be silly. A big bear man like you. You like sweet things, don't you dear?"

Mortimer interjected, "Dotty loves to feed people." Squeezing a large splodge of tapioca into his mouth. "And as for the green door, it leads to the cellar. I would be happy to show you. You should really see the whole house, get a sense of the place."

I sat and ate my pudding silently. I kept thinking of the fairy story of Hansel and Gretel, the letter still hot on my chest. And yet I did not leave. They watched me while I ate. When I had finished, I thought suddenly of my father when I was a boy, and he was warning me not to step too near sleeping crocodiles, because they are not sleeping, they are waiting to catch you.

On the shelf, a beautiful clock caught my eye. It was silver and engraved with fairies dancing round the face. It hummed delicately like an insect.

A dampish hand patted my head, and I looked up at Dotty.

"Come on then, dearie." My head was fuzzy.

I followed her down the hallway and we began to ascend the staircase. Again the brown tobacco-stained wallpaper, a running décor theme throughout the house. A small framed picture of a grey cat called Mr Pickles, no doubt the missing pet, hung near the landing window. And the smell that was lingering in the kitchen but covered up by all that sweetness was much more pungent here. A deep, burnt fatty smell.

Dotty led me into her bedroom. "Here you are, ducky." The room smelt sour. It was again a small room with a large bed with a floral cover. Floral wallpaper and a bedside mirror that had broken.

"Sometimes I hear voices in the walls at night. Chanting and grunting."

The carpet was filthy, cat turds and dust. A framed sepia photo hung above the bed. It was of Dotty as a young girl, tap dancing on Brighton Pier. She looked like a little pixie, a bob of blond curls and twinkling eyes. I got on my knees and looked under the bed. Again, more cat turds, and something else. I reached for it and pulled out a piece of dried human skin with a few hairs sticking out from it.

"Ooh," said Dotty, edging closer, "I wonder what that is. You are staying for dinner, Detective Honey-Flower? I'm making apple pie. Isn't that your favourite?"

"Yes, yes it is my favourite, how did you know that?" I turned to look at her. The piece of dried skin rested like a leaf in the palm of my hand.

"You look like an apple pie sort of man. All big and strong and sweet."

Mortimer popped his head round the corner of the bedroom door. "Found anything interesting?"

"Human skin," I said, holding it out towards him. He glanced down at it momentarily, his eyes then fixing upon me. "And what does this mean for us?"

"This is not a haunting. This is something quite different." I glanced over at the old wardrobe in the corner of Dotty's room and approached it, "May I?" I looked at her and she nodded. The door creaked open theatrically and inside were hung half a dozen moth-eaten dresses with lurid floral patterns. They seemed too big for her. Nothing else there.

I wandered into Mortimer's room, still gripping the skin in my hand like a strange talisman. His room was larger, very dark, without a window. A large bed in the centre of the room which I looked under . No human skin. The room was as hot as an oven. No pictures on the walls, just the same dirty brown wallpaper. Instead of a wardrobe, there was a set of drawers, which I went through. Old pairs of socks, shirts and holey trousers. Again, nothing of interest.

A newspaper was folded in the corner of the room, used as a doorstop. The date caught my eye: *27 December 1881.* I left the room, as I had started sweating. Dotty stepped lightly in front of me on the landing. "I'll make some more tea while you show him the cellar, Mortimer dear."

"A splendid idea." Mortimer led me back down the staircase, past Mr Pickles, the long lost cat. I didn't know what to do with the skin, so I wrapped it in a handkerchief and put it in my pocket. He removed a gold key from his pocket and placed it in the elaborate lock.

"It's a beautiful thing isn't it? The lock." He examined my response.

"It's unusual," I replied.

"Yes, you could say that," and then he winked at me. This took me greatly by surprise. "Tell me," he said, "have you always been a policeman?"

I felt the letter again, warming against my heart, throbbing. "No. I was a boxer in London in my twenties."

"A fighter. I can see that in you."

The door gently opened to reveal a brightly lit, white painted room with a white set of stone washed steps. I had been expecting a dungeon of sorts. But it was almost clinical, a complete contradiction to the rest of the house. We descended the staircase. Hanging on the wall, the only object in the room, was a strange silver clock ticking softly. It has engravings carved round it, intricate human feet and hands. "What do you store in here?" I asked.

"Well, as you can see, nothing at the moment."

"Why is there a lock on the door?"

"To stop you from leaving."

Police Detective Sergeant White
Statement to press officer of The Times
7th October, 1887

A mass grave was discovered at the residence of 7 Dewdrop Lane, South London, yesterday. The incumbent, Mortimer Crumb, and his sister, Dotty, were arrested by Detective Honey-Flower.

So far over one hundred bodies have been recovered from under the floorboards, in the walls and the garden. We ask for anyone with any information to come forward.

VI

Meeting Mr Tumbletee

I was given a two week sabbatical after that experience, and I took a holiday to Norfolk to calm my nerves and visit my Uncle, who was a monk in the Priory of Lowstar, and who had requested my assistance in a private matter.

The path to the Priory was littered with red coloured leaves, some dancing into the air like flames and then falling round my feet, exhausted and extinguished. The mile long walk to the Priory gates stretched out like a great red tongue, surrounded by trees that enclosed it like broken teeth. My Uncle's letter had arrived two days earlier, requesting my assistance in a peculiar situation of which he had supplied me with no information, only an urgency that I attend. I had not seen my Uncle in ten years, and I was both apprehensive and full of happiness, as I had missed him greatly.

The gates of Lowstar Priory manifested behind a thicket of creeping ivy. The small medieval building sat within large gardens of herbs and flowers and a vast expanse of lawn, leading downhill to a lush woodland area. It was beautifully peaceful.

I withdrew a small tin box of sugared pear drops from my pocket and popped a couple in my mouth.

Frederick was standing by the entrance to the Priory, underneath a pouring of wild daisies in a hanging basket. He was tall and strongly built, beardless with a thick head of dark hair. He approached me softly and took my hand in his.

"Goliath, my dear nephew. Thank you so much for coming." The look on his face was of relief and affection. "Come with me, we'll have some tea."

Frederick guided me into the Priory, and led me into the small kitchen, which overlooked the herb garden. The room smelled of honey and spices.

"How was your journey?" He spoke as he guided me to a deep wooden chair around a vast oak table.

"Comfortable, thank you. The scenery, I found very calming. All that flatness."

"Yes," said Frederick, filling a small metal kettle with water and putting it on the stove, "It has an attractive eeriness. but it's not for everyone." He paused and stared at me, sadly. "I can't believe it's been nearly ten years since we last saw each other. I am sorry for it."

"Do you have any biscuits?" I said.

"But you haven't changed, you still have that sweet tooth." He walked over to the cupboard and pulled out a tin. "Custard cream?"

I nodded and he placed them on the table "What has happened, Fred? Tell me."

Frederick stood motionless over the stove. "A few days ago we had a visitor to the Priory. His name was Mr Tumbletee. An eccentric young man. He said he was delivering a gift."

"A gift?" I said, selecting a couple of custard creams.

"Yes, a gift. He had a little black box in his hand, a great big red ribbon around it."

"And who was this gift for?"

Frederick stared at me curiously. "He said it was for you."

The kettle boiled, piercing the air like a banshee. There was a delicate silence between us for a moment. He removed the kettle from the flame and prepared the tea.

"Did you open it?" I finally said as he approached with the tea.

"No, I have kept it safe." He handed me a cup. "I will go and fetch it." And he left the room.

Outside I could see a mangy old white cat lying in the herb garden, its eyes as green and deep as a demon's. It was scratching itself lazily under the rosemary. I sipped my tea and contemplated another custard cream.

Fred returned holding the box, which was a lined with slippery black velvet, and, as he had described, garnished with a large red ribbon bow. He rested it upon the table.

"Did he say anything else to you?"

"No, he just handed me the box and smiled. I noticed he had very bad skin."

I untied the bow, which fell softly aside, and lifted the lid off the box. Inside were ten perfectly preserved white milky human teeth, and a calling card:

Ebeneezer Tumbletee
Travelling Magician & Collector
of Rare Antiquities

Frederick looked horrified and stepped back across the kitchen floor. "Get that thing out of here, now."

I followed his wishes and disposed of the box. I walked a half a mile from the Priory to a little stone bridge, and dropped the foul gift into the waters, watching it carried downstream. My hands were clenched and sweating and my heart felt as though it had been squashed by a fist.

When I returned to the Priory, he was waiting for an explanation. I felt physically sick. I sat back down in the chair in the kitchen while he hovered above me, furious.

"I am so sorry," I said, my head in my hands. "I have no idea why this has happened."

"You're a policeman. You must have enemies, Goliath," Fred muttered. "Who have you angered?"

"I don't know. I've never been sent teeth before."

There was the sound of a horse and carriage and we both looked up at one another. We walked to the door, where outside stood a blood red carriage and a cabby, a young man with bright orange hair who approached us gingerly. "My name is Foxhole. I am here to collect Detective Honey-Flower. An invitation from Mr Tumbletee, Esquire." He had a wicked little grin upon his face.

"Don't get in that carriage," Fredrick boomed and stood in my path, and he glared at Foxhole, "And as for you, sir, I don't appreciate your master's vile gifts."

Foxhole stepped back and muttered something inaudible under his breath. I put my hand on Fredrick's shoulder. "Let me go. I have to find out what he wants."

Foxhole opened the carriage door. "In you pop, sir."

Frederick stared at me. "Are you mad? What power do these people have over you?"

"Please, Fred. You have to trust me. Send a telegram to Detective Sergeant White. Inform him of what has happened."

"I'll have him back by midnight, sir. Just like Cinderella," smirked Foxhole.

"You better," demanded my uncle, and turned to me. "I will be waiting for you."

I stepped into the carriage, which was lined with red silk. Fred watched me leave. He looked so worried for me.

We drove off down the beautiful red mile leading out of the Priory grounds, while the little black box floated downstream gently on silver notes of water.

We drove for an hour while the sun descended – an orange melting into the flat frying pan landscape. Foxhole remained silent, occasionally glancing over at me with his curious little dark eyes.

Finally, the carriage stopped. The sky outside was

inky black and dotted with stars. Foxhole opened the door.

"Where are we?" I said.

He had a mouth like a slit in a moneybox. "Your dinner reservation."

We were standing in a large flat field. In the centre was a table laid for dinner, with a candle burning and a bottle of red wine. A heavy, fat moon sat over us, providing a luminescent light, as though a theatrical backdrop. Seated at the table was a young, slim gentleman dressed in an elegant dinner jacket, his top hat resting on the ground. As I approached him, he rose and our eyes met. His face was moon glow white with black eyes and a pox-scared complexion. His hair stardust white. He looked half fairy, half demon.

"Welcome, Goliath Honey-Flower." He spoke softly and gestured to me to sit while he poured out the wine. Foxhole wandered back to the carriage. I wondered whose field we were sitting in and whether a disgruntled farmer would suddenly appear, shotgun in hand, upon discovering two gentleman having dinner. He might get the wrong idea.

"Did you enjoy the teeth?" He sipped from his wine glass. I considered for a moment that he was perhaps completely insane.

"What do you want from me, Mr Tumbletee?" I refrained from drinking the wine.

"You interest me, Mr Honey-Flower."

"What on Earth are you talking about?" I fumed.

"You destroyed the Crumb Siblings – my little project. I had invested a great deal of time and energy in them both and you put an end to it. You have been an inconvenience to me. And you have been noticed." His eyes rolled upwards.

"They were mass murderers and they tried to eat me," I said, disgusted, banging my fist heavily on the table. It shook violently, the wine bottle nearly falling off. Tumbletee stepped forward and leaned over me and whispered, "They were my pet project. You spoiled my fun."

I stood up and squared with him. I was huge in comparison to him. I was built like a wall and a foot taller. His face cracked into a slight smile and he delicately stepped back. "It's like you've been carved from a rock. You're a force of nature. But you will stop your meddling into my affairs in future or I will be forced to deal with you."

"You give me no choice but to arrest you–"

He interrupted me. "You will do no such thing," and pointed a gun at my head. "Now sit down and we'll discuss this like gentlemen, there's a good boy."

"You're ma–"

He interrupted me again. "Mad... Yes, of course I'm mad. Do you think a sane person would collect human teeth? Of course not, it's just not rational. Now calm yourself. As I was saying, I really don't want to have to shoot you. Call this a friendly warning." He smiled and it was ghastly.

"What are you?" I said, dumbfounded.

"Now that is an interesting question." He opened his mouth wide.

"You're not going to sing, are you?"

"You're a funny man, detective. No, I wasn't about to break into song, although I have a great fondness for musical expression in all its forms."

"WHO ARE YOU?" I bellowed, pounding my fists on the table, the wine bottle shattering on the ground.

He stood up. "I am the game, detective. I am the game."

"I want to return to my Uncle now," I said. "I have nothing else to say to you."

I turned to leave and walked towards the carriage, where Foxhole was leaning mischievously, trying to earwig on the night air.

Tumbletee called out to me. "It's been a delight. We must do this again soon," he said, placing his top hat on his head and bowing like an actor on a stage, his audience the dead planet that hung above him in the cosmic stalls.

VII

Tumbletee in London

I travelled back to London. The trial of Mortimer and Dotty Crumb was headlining the newspapers. Their faces peered out from the pages like ghosts trapped within glass.

I returned to work, where a handful of parcels were waiting for me. Beautifully wrapped boxes, each with a set of human teeth.

Mr Tumbletee would not leave me alone. I took them in to show Detective Sergeant Percival White and I sat in his office while he examined them carefully, and I explained the story.

"How many of these gifts have you received, Goliath?" His fingers cupped the little box.

"So far – half a dozen, sir."

"After your telegram I put out some general inquiries on Tumbletee, to see if anyone has heard of him. Hopefully some information should materialise soon. This is an obsessive, strange individual. Take no chances, Goliath. I shall send out a constable outside your lodgings tonight. Fellow named Walnut, very reliable. Keep me informed if any other nasty little parcels arrive. He sounds like a showman to me. He wants a reaction. Don't give it to him. Let's draw him out."

"What do you think he wants with me?"

Detective Sergeant White put the box of teeth back on the table. "He is of course completely insane. He likes to play games. You ruined one of his games, and so now you must play."

That evening I spent with Constable Walnut outside my lodgings. I watched him from the small attic window. He would occasionally stare at the stars, whistling, and this made me like him. I used to do that as a boy in Cairo. He also seemed to like his food very much, as he had several packs of sandwiches and a large slab of plum cake in his pocket. I took him out some hot tea, which pleased him.

"Thank you, sir," he replied, traces of cake around his lips.

"Anything suspicious?" I asked.

"No, no sign of the lunatic, sir. Man with a limp

earlier, couple of stray dogs, but nothing more to report."

"I really am grateful for this. Thank you."

"My pleasure. The stars are out. Very bright. Lovely evening, really. If the tooth collecting fruitcake appears, sir, I'll have him."

"Thank you, Walnut," and I returned to my lodgings, where a small box with a red ribbon rested on the step.

The following morning brought some results from Detective Sergeant White's inquiries into Mr Tumbletee. An elderly lady was waiting with information in White's office. She sat hunched over the desk, wearing a filthy lacy brown dress with matching grubby gloves. Her face was spider-lined and also grey with a mass of white hair piled high on her head, and rotten black teeth. She smelt foul, the bottom of the Thames foul. Detective Sergeant White and I sat opposite her and he opened the line of questioning.

"Thank you for coming. May I ask your name?"

The lips of the creature moved, slightly wonky. "Alice Butters."

"Can you please tell me something about yourself?"

"Why?" she asked mockingly, her little dark eyes

fixed upon him like a goblin.

"I like to know where I am getting my information from."

She relented. "I work at the Bluebell Tavern off Mitre Square. Serving drinks, cleaning. That sort of thing. Landlord lets me sleep in the cellar. Got my own bed. I have no family. All dead. Just me."

I thought her an odd little creature.

Detective Sergeant White watched her coolly. "What do you know about Mr Tumbletee, Alice?"

"Well, I've seen him before. He's been in the pub a couple of times. Very elegant dresser. A real gentleman. But he frightens off the girls 'cause of his face."

"His face?" Detective Sergeant White remarked.

"Yes. He's had the pox or something. Bad skin and white as the moon, sir. He left his business card with the landlord, said something about selling antiquities," and at this she handed it over, exactly the same as the one I had been given.

"Did he mention his work, or where he lived in London?"

"He said he was a collector, sir, of unusual artefacts. Said he travelled a lot, mostly abroad, and had come back to England for some unsettled business."

"Which was?"

"He didn't say, sir. But he said he was lodging with a Mrs Pudding round the corner."

At this remark Detective Sergeant White opened the door and called Constable Walnut in. He spoke quietly in his ear and then sat down again.

"You sending your hounds off to sniff him out, detective?" Mrs Butters asked.

"Something like that," he replied. "Now what else do you know? Any small detail may be important."

"What has he done, exactly, if I may ask?" she peered at him curiously.

"He's someone with whom I would very much like to have a conversation."

"He sounds like a bad boy to me. A very bad boy…" and she began to cackle, to laugh. That black mouth, with green gums and brown teeth. I felt ill looking at that mouth.

"Is there anything else, Mrs Butters?"

She kept laughing.

"Mrs Butters?" Detective Sergeant White repeated coldly.

The laughing stopped suddenly and those little dark eyes looked down at her own hands and played with the dirty brown lace over her fingers. "I would say he's as mad as a hat. I really can tell you nothing more, gentlemen."

She stood to leave, Detective Sergeant White escorting her to the entrance, down a long, narrow corridor. She stood by the door and turned to look at me sideways and bowed very low. And then, smiling like a wicked goblin, she disappeared out of the door and into the busy street.

I stood there, my feet planted in the carpet. Rooted to the floor. My brain dumb. And then I shouted, "IT'S HIM. IT'S HIM!"

But he was already lost in London.

My name is Ebeneezer Tumbletee and I am a puzzle box. I am an emporium of magic tricks. I am the saw that the magician cuts his assistant in half with. And then people wonder why she's dead.

I am a nasty thing and as *mad as* **scissors** .

Snip snip snip snip

Tumbletee.

That is my name.

And you ask me, what is my story, where am I from? Am I even human? And I shall tell you. Yes, yes, I was once human, but I was never nice.

I was raised by a wealthy family in London. My

father was a merchant in jewels and made a fortune travelling the world. I was an only child, independent and bright, and it was thought I would take over my father's business when I came of age. My father would bring home pockets stuffed with pearls and emeralds as big as eyeballs. And I would juggle them – play with a king's treasure like a court jester. I was given everything I could ever want and yet I still turned out wrong.

I killed all our family pets, threw their bodies in the sewers, but I kept the teeth as a souvenir. Stuffed them in the velvet jewellery boxes my father brought back from his trip to Paris. Diamonds were replaced by teeth. My collection was kept at the bottom of my wardrobe. Row upon row of little black boxes. Little magic boxes for a wicked fairy.

By the time I was ten years old I had killed my first human being. It was our serving maid. I pushed her down the stairs. ha ha ha ha ha ha ha HA HA HA HA HA

It was easy enough. And her teeth were my prize. Despite my deformity of the mind, my family remained blissfully unaware. I sometimes wonder if they were completely stupid. I managed to commit seven murders before my fifteenth birthday, one of which included my cousin, Septimus, to whom befell an unfortunate accident. He slipped and fell off the roof. My foot firmly planted in his backside. **Tee hee hee!!** It was all far too easy and far too enjoyable for me to ever be able to stop.

Our house was a lavish but gloomy three storey building near Hyde Park, which my bedroom window overlooked. I would watch the pedestrians and think of ways to get their teeth. You may wonder why I had such an obsession for teeth. I have often wondered myself and I really don't have a clue. I cannot give you an answer. My first memory of teeth was my grandfather's. I was sitting perched on his knee, my face close to his mouth, which was covered in grey whiskers. And his teeth were huge and yellow fang-like monstrosities. Incisors like a sabre-toothed tiger. I remember thinking, he's going to take a bite out of me.

And now you're wondering if I now have those specimens in one of my little dark boxes don't you? Well, the answer is yes. They have always been my prize possession. I didn't kill him. He died peacefully in his armchair. I just pulled them out later.

But things change, they always do, and my life just after my fifteenth birthday changed dramatically.

My father had been away for several months in Africa, overseeing a diamond mining operation, and he returned unexpectedly one evening with a terrible fever, with pustules on his face and body, sweating and hallucinating. The doctor confined him to his room, but it was far too late.

The next day my mother contracted the disease, followed by myself. My father died on the third day, screaming. We let the servants go. The doctors could do nothing; they could not recognize the disease. I lay in my room and I could hear my mother crying next door, dying. During the night she passed away and I was left alone. I did not want to die. I did not want to end. I kept thinking I could see my grandfather sitting in the corner of the room watching me, smiling and toothless. He smelt of boiled butterscotch sweets. I think he was happy watching me die. I think he was chuckling.

And so I said out loud, "My name is Ebeneezer Tumbletee and I will make a deal with any angel or devil to save my life."

I didn't get an angel. But I wasn't expecting one. And he appeared and stood by my bed with his little black spectacles and introduced himself as the Lord of the Underworld.

"You are a curious thing, Ebeneezer," he said,

leaning against the wardrobe. I could barely keep my eyes open; a haze was forming around the room, dark and smoggy. My grandfather had disappeared.

"I think you had better come with me. And don't worry, I won't bite," he said, smiling.

I am a magician. I am a collector of rare artefacts, especially teeth. And I had one particular artefact I wished to sell. A soul. A very rare soul. I kept it in a beautiful glass jar. The soul was a wispy trail of blue, swirling and bubbling. I was sad to part with it, but there were other things I required.

I visited the clockmaker, Albert Chimes. The extender of lives, the killer of children. I had a trade for him. *A soul for teeth,* *a soul for teeth,* *a soul for teeth –* **toothypegs**.

"Good morning, Albert," I said, and took off my top hat. He looked positively terrified and this pleased me. I was perhaps the one thing that frightened him.

"What are you doing here, Tumbletee?" I had

traded with him before, he knew what I liked.

"I have something to sell. Something that might interest you," and I removed the jar from my coat pocket and put it into his hands. His eyes lit up, mesmerized by the contents.

"A soul."

"A very unusual soul," I replied.

"How did you acquire this?"

"It is from an Egyptian princess. I spent some time on an excavation in Cairo. Her tomb was painted with red flowers. Her soul lay in a little pot waiting to be collected."

"This soul is not human. It is something else," Albert muttered, shaking it slightly. He was excited. I could see his hands trembling.

"Yes, she was rather unusual. Some sort of sorceress, perhaps? Put her into one of your clocks."

And then I spied a beautiful grandfather clock engraved with ladybirds, at the back of his shop. "Something appropriate. Something like that," and I pointed at it.

"And what do you want in exchange?"

I smiled. "Teeth. Teeth of the children. I need rather a lot."

"What do you want with the teeth?" He looked disgusted.

I laughed out loud. "You have the audacity to ask me what I need children's teeth for, and yet you kill them and stuff their souls into clocks. Give me the teeth, Albert, there's a good boy, and you can have the soul."

"Very well," he rasped, and a deal was struck.

"How shall I get the teeth to you?"

"My manservant Foxhole will come and collect. I need a rather large supply."

"Of course, but I will need a little time to get it ready for you." And he examined the soul as a schoolboy looking at a jar of sweets. "Wonderful," he sighed.

"I thought you'd like her."

The Mermaid's Tail sliced through the waves. Taking us back to England, back to the ladybird clock. Back to my mad grandfather. Back to the beginning, to find an ending.

I peered over the edge of the boat into green waters, saw a flash of silver fin. Closed my eyes and imagined an underwater city with pyramids tangled in black seaweeds, the priests float through their temples with fish tails and algae frilled eyes. I dipped my hand into sea foam, icing on a great salty cake. I smell shipwrecks and shark bites. But Captain Mackerel is favoured by the old Gods; he wears bone charms round his neck and kisses mermaids. We are safe with him.

Goliath and Captain Mackerel play chess at night. Captain Mackerel always wins (I think his cat helps him, for cats know about hidden things, they can smell secrets). It purred and flicked its tail, expecting a boiled herring. I stroked its back, stared into its giant jewelled eyes. "What sort of magic cat are you?" I asked it.

It replied with a sly wink and leapt off my lap into shadows, in search of rats.

At night, Goliath told me fairy stories; princesses and peas, kissing frogs and bad tempered wizards. I liked to hear about the wizards; their funny pointy hats, their wands that zap, their long blue beards and unicorn horn shaped towers. Spiral to the top. Point at stars like a pyramid. I miss Egypt, I tell Goliath and pull his wild beard.

"We will return, little one," he says, and I fall asleep, my little fist still clutching his great beard. Taking him with me into dreams.

IX

August 1888
THE CHASE FOR TUMBLETEE

My grandmother Isabella told me once that there are plenty of funny buggers in London. That gem of wisdom was given to me while she was peeling spuds. She said "men are like potatoes – occasionally you come across a rotten one, or one that looks suspicious."

Constable Walnut and I were on the trail for Tumbletee, and if he were a potato my grandmother would have slung him in with the pig slops. We had located the landlady, Mrs Pudding, off Mitre Square.

"Do you think he will be dressed up as a woman again, sir?" said Walnut.

"Be prepared for any eventuality, Walnut," I replied.

The lodgings were small and run down. A very short, plump woman in a mourning gown let us in.

"Mrs Pudding?" I enquired.

"Yes," she said.

"My name is Detective Sergeant White and this is Constable Walnut. Do you have a tenant named Ebeneezer Tumbletee?"

"I do, and he's a very fine gentleman."

"May we see his room, madam?"

She took a brass key out of her pocket. "You may, but you're interrupting my mourning of my late husband, Mr Pudding, who died at sea."

"My condolences, madam," and we followed her up a flight of creaky stairs to the attic rooms.

"Shark," she added.

"Where?" said Walnut and looked worried.

"My husband was eaten by a shark." Mrs Pudding crossed herself.

We arrived at Tumbletee's room.

"He's been a very good tenant. Quiet, pays his rent on time, polite and well behaved. I couldn't ask for any more. He's a perfect example of what I expect in a tenant."

She placed the key in the lock and the door swung open. The room was covered in blood. It was all over the floors and up the walls and on the ceiling. Mrs Pudding screamed and fainted into the arms of Constable Walnut, who buckled under her weight.

I stood looking into the room. On the bed, which was saturated in gore, was a little box tied with a black ribbon. It was the only object in the room not bloodstained. I moved closer and picked it up. It was the size of my fist. I opened it. A row of human teeth sat at the bottom of the box, and a small piece of paper on which there was writing:

Dear Detective Sergeant White,

Meet me for a little chat at the British Museum, 2pm today in the Egyptian exhibition.

Your faithful friend,

Ebeneezer Tumbletee Esq.

I informed Constable Walnut and left him with Mrs Pudding to take a brief statement. I left immediately for the British Museum, as I had less than an hour before my appointment. Walnut would follow shortly. The sky was already beginning to cloud over; thin eel-like swirls painted the sky.

The Museum was quiet and empty. I counted only a handful of people. I walked past a series of Roman statues, each one smooth and cream-coloured, watching over me softly. My feet tapping, echoing on the stone floors.

The Egyptian exhibition was on the second floor. I could see three people hovering about: a little girl and her mother, holding hands, peering at a gold and turquoise tureen within a cabinet with crocodile engravings. And a curate with red hair, and a large, equally red nose was touching the black sarcophagus in the centre of the room, where a young king slept in death. I could hear the little girl speaking to her mother, "Why do they like crocodiles so much, Mummy? Crocodiles eat people."

I stood next to the curate, "Hello, Mr Tumbletee." I knew it was him. I knew he wouldn't be able to resist it again.

The curate turned, grinning manically. "Oh, well done, detective. So you met Mrs Pudding?"

"Yes."

"She's in mourning, you know. So I hope you were sensitive with her."

I said nothing.

"Of course," he continued, "He's been dead over fifteen years, so she needs to get over it at some point."

"I have to arrest you, Tumbletee."

"Have you ever been to Egypt, Detective Sergeant White?"

"No."

"It's a fascinating place. I was over there for quite a few months, travelling and acquiring objects from excavations. Do you know much about the Egyptian gods?"

"Mr Tumbletee, we need to go down to the station to have this conversation. Other constables will be arriving shortly."

"There is a god called Apophis. He's comes from the underworld. He's a snake god, but more importantly he's a force of chaos. I like chaos. The body or coils of this snake god represent a void or black hole that swallows people up. Do you know what I am saying to you, Detective Sergeant White?"

"I think I know what you are."

"Very good. We understand one another. There is absolutely no question of redemption or remorse for me.

I **am chaos**. I am a **black h**O**le**.

I will not stop unless someone is capable of stopping me."

Constable Walnut arrived. "Everything alright, sergeant?"

"Yes, Walnut, everything is in hand. Mr Tumbletee was just about to accompany us to the police station."

"Let's be having you then, you funny bugger," Constable Walnut approached.

"Ahh, Constable Walnut. The comedy sidekick."

"I'm not the one who dresses up as a member of the clergy with a rubber nose," Walnut replied, waggling a finger in protestation.

"Are you capable of stopping me?" Mr Tumbletee looked directly at me and then opened his hands. "Did I tell you I was a *magician?*"

And he disappeared.

"What the hell?' cried Walnut.

"Seal off the exits to the museum. He must be here somewhere," I cried.

But he wasn't.

A few days later a letter arrived for me, postmarked Paris:

Dear Detective Sergeant White,

Paris is beautiful this time of year. I am sorry we couldn't have got to know each other better.

I have a little project I want to begin. It involves

BUTCHERING women. So you'll know when I
have returned. Don't try and arrest me next
time, Percival. Just kill me.

With love,

　　Tumbletee

X

August 1888
MR TUMBLETEE & MR FINGERS
HAVE DINNER

It was raining in Paris, and late evening. The moon and stars were dazzling. I don't usually notice them at all, but it was hard not to that night. They were so bright. Spermy wriggling shooting stars fell, white across a black canvas. I was meeting my father for dinner. It had been a while since we'd met, but we'd a lot to talk about, and I could already smell him. He was underneath the earth, deep, deep down where the secret stains oozed. Mushroom spores, broken glass, hands of women, bones of a saint. He's a forbidden land and I am his map. See the ink stains in my eyes?

I'd chosen a dark little restaurant and a candlelit table in a secretive corner. A bottle of champagne, and I'd ordered bloodied beef and custard apple tarts for pudding. Not that he liked that kind of food.

Neither did I, really. His wafty scent mingled with the Parisian moonlight – it was dried blood, it was dark earth and cogs turning on his ancient clocks. **Daddy DADDY DADDY daddy DADDY DADDY MY DADDY MY DADDY MY DADDY MY DADDY DADDY DADDY.**

Daddy of the Underworld.

Ladybird waistcoat, dark spectacles, crooked smile. He sat and poured himself a glass of champagne.

"Ebeneezer, my boy. It's lovely to see you again."

"Father. I was hoping we could talk."

"I've been keeping track of your career. Very interesting. Very. Interesting," He sipped his champagne. I could tell he was angry and it pleased me.

"I want you to be impressed, Father."

"You gave a soul to Albert Chimes, the clockmaker. Why?"

"I have no use for souls."

"Do you know what that soul was?"

"I knew it was unusual. Some sort of witch princess."

"Did you realise the power it had?"

"No." **Lying,** *tee hee!*

"Then let me tell you, boy," and he forced a forkful of bloodied beef into his mouth and chewed. "That soul is able to open doorways to other worlds and to control time. The Egyptian princess had enormous power. You gave that soul to a grubby little clockmaker in the East End of London, who will stick it in a clock. I must now retrieve it for myself."

"As you wish, Father."

"You enjoy your costumes a little too much; I did not pick an actor for a son."

"What a shame. I thought I was entertaining you."

"You have no sense of control."

"I want to destroy things. **Break them apart**," and I stared into him.

"I did not raise my son to be chaotic."

"No, you raised me to be like you. Part of the void, Daddy."

He poured more champagne for us both. "I saved you from death, Ebeneezer. I gave you a new home, a new life. In future I want you to be more controlled. I do not want to be embarrassed. These silly games you play. You are no longer a child. Kill what you want, who you want, but remember who you are. You are sending a message. I will not have you dressing up in women's clothes again."

"I was very convincing."

"If you embarrass me again I will cut you off without a second thought. Do you understand me?"

"You wouldn't dare."

"Ebeneezer. No more dressing up, no more games, no more chaos. You must have control over what you are, or you will fall into madness."

"I am already mad, Father."

He didn't answer me, and then ate some more of the beef. "Every action you take represents me. You are my assassin and you must behave in a manner I see fitting."

"What do you want from me?"

"You will leave these London policeman alone. You will concentrate on your work. I am eager to hear your next project."

"Yes, yes. I was thinking of prostitutes, knives and a doctor's bag. I thought souvenirs could be taken and eaten."

Daddy smiled deeply. "I like that very much, very much. How will you kill them?"

"Scissor knife slashing!" And I slice my beef to show him.

"Good. It sends a clear message." He wiped his lips with his napkin. "If you play childish games again with the policeman you will be on your own. I will not tolerate any more silliness. Do you understand me?"

"Yes, Father."

We began to eat the pudding with custard. Great creamy dollops. Each mouthful a sin.

PART FOUR

My house, my father's house, is full of demons.
Stuffed full of them. Sweeties in a jam jar.

This simply will not do.

My name is John Loveheart
and I was not born wicked.

**Loveheart Loveheart Loveheart Loveheart
Loveheart**
I hold the pistol to Mr Fingers' brain.
**Loveheart Loveheart Loveheart Loveheart
Loveheart**
You will remember my name.

I shoot him in the head. His brain explodes all
over the wall.

He's not happy about it.

Whilst his brain reforms, I shoot a few of the monsters in dinner suits. Heads bursting like tomatoes over my beautiful wallpaper.

"YOU WOULD BETRAY ME? YOU STUPID LITTLE BOY!"

I reply as restrained as possible. "Get out of *my* house or I will use your skull as a vase."

"I AM YOUR FATHER. HOW DARE YOU SPEAK TO ME LIKE THAT?"

"You're not my father. You're an imposter." I shoot Doctor Cherrytree, who is trying to sneak off like a snivelling coward. He screams and falls dead on the floor.

The sea of monsters grabs me. His vile acquaintances.

"Hold him!" shrieks Mr Fingers. "You're finished, Loveheart." And he moves his hand towards my throat.

I look over to Mirror. "I'm so sorry," I say to her.

A great eagle flies through the window, smashing glass and circles the demons, screeching. It is her protector. A loud pounding at the door sounds, then it bursts open.

Death walks into the room.

"I am sorry for intruding," the boy says, softly. His

voice has a supernatural quality, and he smells of formaldehyde. Mr Fingers knows who he is. He knows – and he is worried.

The boy continues, "You appear to be having a party. I rarely get invited to parties. I tend to spoil them."

"What do you want?" Mr Fingers looks distinctly uncomfortable.

"We had a little discussion, if I recall. You are not going to eat her. You are not going to increase your power."

"*How dare you!* What gives you the right to tell me what to do?" cries Mr Fingers.

"Because I am older than Time, I am the great equalizer. You will do what I say or I will EVAPORATE YOU."

A great muttering among the guests, and I am released.

"No!" Mr Fingers screams, "NO NO NO NO NO NO NO NO NO!"

The boy raises his hands gently in the air and the monsters in dinner jackets start to crumble into dust, one by one like a sea wave. I unlock the cage and carry the woman Mirror in my arms.

"What are you doing?" screams Mr Fingers, "She is my food!"

The eagle circles him, screeching. A great mirror hangs on the wall behind him, and the glass is starting to shift and move like water. She is doing something. The great eagle claws at his face, screeching wildly. She is staring into the mirror and it is opening like a doorway. She raises her hand and he is sucked into it. His scream is like a child. He tries to smash his way out but he's locked in there.

She looks out at the remaining guests and they start to explode like champagne corks. Heads popping off.

This is all rather fun.

The eagle circles the room.

Death watches and I am laughing. I sit Mirror on my father's chair. The blood is filling up the room. I stand on the table of the feast and laugh at the corpses.

All is suddenly quiet. Mirror is stroking the eagle's head as though they are lovers. It is over. My kingdom has been returned to me. I can hear Mr Fingers behind me, banging on the mirror, and I wave at him. The lady and the eagle move to leave. Mirror approaches Death.

"Thank you," she says.

"My pleasure," he replies.

Then she turns to look at me. "Mr Loveheart.

You're a wicked, wonderful hero." She turns away and strides out of my kingdom.

Goodbye, Lady Mirror. If I stare into you for too long I see my face. I see the colour of my eyes.

"Do come back and visit," I shout, kicking a severed hand from the table. I stare down at Death, who is surrounded by pieces of corpses.

"Please help yourself to the buffet."

And he does.

"The jam tarts are excellent," says Death.

October 1888
MIRROR & GOLIATH

We are back in Cairo with Goliath's father. We sit drinking coffee in the shade and eating honey cakes, the sun lemon-hot outside.

Goliath's father has given me a present: a copy of the Brothers Grimm fairy tales with hand-drawn illustrations. They are dark and beautiful. Children hiding in the woods, wolf eyes peering through trees, water flowers drifting lazily on the stream and gingerbread houses. All in my hands. All in my hands.

I feel safe in Egypt. I feel as though I am home. The excavation of the tomb of the princess is now complete. We went to visit it, so many months work, but Goliath's father has restored and uncovered so much beauty. Above the ceiling of her tomb are tiny stars; the sarcophagus is made of gold with turquoise jewels. I stroke it with my hand; it is cool and familiar. Why do I feel so comfortable in this place? I try to imagine what the princess was like. Was she beautiful? Was she full of deep magic? Goliath's father tells us she had her own temple and hundreds of priests. He has started to uncover her temple, his new project. I am not allowed to visit this site, as it is too dangerous, beams are holding up parts of the temple and Goliath fears for my safety and the baby, so I must wait. I must wait to see her temple.

A postcard arrives for me. It has a silken embroidery of a big red heart stuck to one side.

Dear Miss Mirror,

I wanted to say how terribly sorry I am that you were nearly eaten in my house. I have been thinking about you a great deal. Mr Fingers has been thinking about you too – he's still stuck in the mirror and I'm not letting him out. Bad Daddy! I suppose I am bored without you – if I had any servants I would give them a good thrashing. Ha ha ha ha ha ha ha ha ha.

Your devoted servant

Mr Loveheart 🖤

I decide to send Mr Loveheart a photograph of the excavation of the tomb of the princess. I look at the heaps of photographs and sketches Goliath's father has made. There are sketches of the pots, frogs leaping over water, dragonflies darting over reeds and a crocodile lazily sleeping in the sun. There are photographs of the walls of her tomb; one shows the moon hanging over the Nile while black dogs stare up at it, transfixed and howling. Another shows the red flowers bursting from the princess's mouth, spewing out like flames.

I then examine photographs of the people excavating the tombs, men with shovels and lanterns. Sweat, dust and machinery. One of Goliath's father with bright, curious eyes and a big beaming smile as he finds the entrance to the tomb. Another shows him deciphering the hieroglyphics on the tomb wall, which depicts frogs leaping into the air and turning into stars. Then at the bottom of the pile I see a picture of the sarcophagus of the princess, and Goliath's father and another man standing by it. This other man has stark white hair and a face pitted like the moon. In his hands is a little pot. Goliath's father and he are shaking hands. The name at the bottom reads *Tumbletee*. This is the photograph I choose to send Mr Loveheart and I am not sure why I have chosen it.

Dear Mr Loveheart,
*   I forgive you. Please keep Mr Fingers in the*
mirror. Wave at him often and send my fondest
regards. I send you this picture of the tomb of the
princess. There is a man called Tumbletee in the
picture, and for some reason I keep thinking you
should know him.
*   I don't think we will ever meet again, Mr*
Loveheart, so I hope you find happiness.
*   Love,*
*   Mirror*

I send it straight away. And I know I will never
hear from him again.

The moon this evening is enormous. The three of
us sit round the table eating honeyed lamb and
drinking wine. Goliath is helping his father excavate
the temple of the princess. They are both so excited
as they have already found a secret chamber and a
sacrificial alter. Goliath touches my face with his
great hand and he tells me tomorrow he will take
me to see outside the temple and see the artefacts
they have retrieved.

"What sort of sacrifices were made in her temple?" I ask.

Goliath's father replies very animatedly, "It looks as though it was human sacrifice. Mirrors were used. We found fragments of them with black obsidian handles. Very beautiful. Her priests wore long robes with masks that looked like insects."

"Insects?" I say.

"Yes. They looked like ladybirds."

October 1888
ICABOD TIDDLE

It is the most beautiful day, and I am sitting in my garden with my pipe and my notebook, writing a new fairy story. The papers are still full of tales of Jack the Ripper, how he might be dressing up as a sailor, a soldier, a doctor. Costumes, games, riddle-like letters to the police, missing livers, missing hearts. There's a real fairy tale villain. There's a real monster.

Horace and the Magic Foot was, thank heavens, burnt on the fire. I feel I can write what I want now, whether the publisher wants it or not.

I'm not writing shit any more. I won't do it.

October 1888
DETECTIVE SERGEANT WHITE
& CONSTABLE WALNUT

I'm in Brighton, sitting on the beach, enjoying a cup of tea. Sitting about twenty yards from me is a jewel thief called Perkins, whom I've followed from London. It's taken weeks to track him but it should soon all be worthwhile. Patience is a virtue. Constable Walnut brings over a couple of ice creams.

"Is he doing anything, Sir?"

"No, he's waiting like us."

"Chocolate or vanilla?" says Walnut.

"Vanilla please," and he hands it to me, melting round my fingers.

"Well, it's a lovely day for catching criminals," says Walnut.

And then we see another figure walking across the sands. He's wearing a purple velvet jacket covered in red love hearts.

"Here comes trouble," sighs Walnut.

Mr Loveheart approaches Perkins, who's sitting dipping his toes in the sea. He takes out a long silver sword and with one swoop Perkins' head flies off into the ocean.

"Oh for God's sake," I cry.

Mr Loveheart comes running over, smiling, and hands me a bag full of stolen emeralds.

"Believe me, Detective Sergeant White, he deserved to die. Nasty piece of work that one. Strangled his grandmother."

"Why are you here, Mr Loveheart?"

"Well, it's about that little favour you said you would do for me."

"Go on," I say, and lick the remainder of my ice cream.

"You must let me kill Tumbletee. No police interference. He is mine to play with."

Mr Fingers

I am trapped in an eight foot tall mirror. It may as well be a coffin. I scream, I lick my tongue up and down the glass, and my boy watches me and laughs.

It may as well be a coffin.

Aunt Eva

I have been thinking again about that boy who broke my heart when I was seventeen. I have been questioning myself, questioning whether my actions were fair. I murdered him and ate his heart as an act of vengeance. Why do I always end up thinking about him? Why do I go back to the same memories, interrogate myself?

Because I loved him. Because I loved him. Because I loved him.

November 1888
MR TUMBLETEE

I am dressed up as a doctor with my bag of knives.
Slice and dice.

Slice and dice
slice and dice
slice and dice.

I'm afraid Daddy disowned me after the last girl.
I was beginning to embarrass him. I made rather a
lot of mess. But I saved him the heart.

I'm bored now of this game. Want to play another.

A gentleman strolls past me and looks at me
oddly.

I scream, "I will see your head in a bucket!"

I think I have become madness. I have melted
into it like cream into hot chocolate, far too easily.
The man has disappeared. I walk back to my

lodgings, the fog thick and soupy. I walk across London Bridge; I can hear the clinking of blades in my black bag. Shiny crocodile teeth.

There's a man standing on the other side of the bridge. He's wearing funny-looking clothing. He's dressed in black like me, but with red love hearts all over him like a disease. He has a long blade in his hands, silver like the moon. I walk towards him, step closer to this strange creature until I can see his face. He has black eyes, like me, and he is grinning.

"Hello, brother," he says.

"Loveheart, it's been such a very long time. I have missed you, baby brother," and I draw my long knife out of my black bag. It glints like a celebrity. "Every star has its counterpoint, every wormhole in space its twin. And you are mine."

"I'm going to stick your head on a pole outside Loveheart Manor," he replies.

"Oh, really! I shall slice you up like a Battenberg. It's such a shame – we are so similar, Loveheart. Why kill me?"

"Because I have standards," he says.

Mr Loveheart

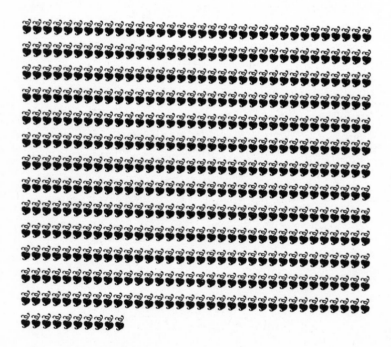

Death

Time for the ending. I like the happy ones the best.

THE END

Acknowledgments

Big thank you to Bryony Woods, Lee Harris, and Marc Gascoigne and the rest of the Angry Robot team. A special mention for Sean Bean (especially in medieval costume and wielding a massive sword), and for chocolate!

About the Author

Ishbelle Bee writes horror and she loves fairy tales, the Victorian period (especially top hats!), and cake tents at village fêtes (she believes serial killers usually opt for the Victoria Sponge). She currently lives in Edinburgh, in Scotland. She doesn't own a rescue cat, but if she did his name would be Mr Pickles. Her next book will be *The Contrary Tale of the Butterfly Girl*.

twitter.com/IshbelleBee

SOMETIMES, ONE MUST
DO THE UNTHINKABLE...

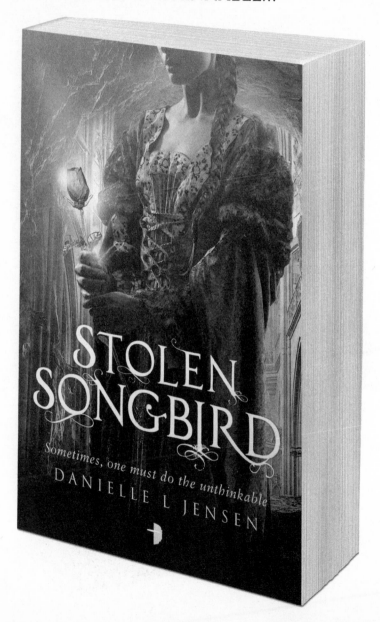

STOLEN
SONGBIRD

Sometimes, one must do the unthinkable

DANIELLE L JENSEN

HIDDEN HUNTRESS

Sometimes, one must accomplish the impossible

DANIELLE L JENSEN

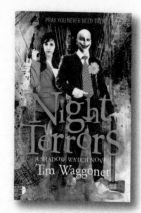

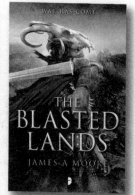

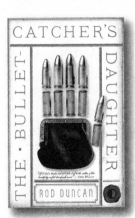